DOGSONG

DOGSONG

·

Gary Paulsen

ALADDIN PAPERBACKS

First Aladdin Paperbacks edition October 1995
Copyright © 1985 by Gary Paulsen

Aladdin Paperbacks
An imprint of Simon & Schuster
Children's Publishing Division
1230 Avenue of the Americas
New York, NY 10020

The text of this book was set in 12-point Janson.
Manufactured in the United States of America

The Library of Congress has cataloged the hardcover
edition as follows:
Paulsen, Gary. Dogsong.
Summary: A fourteen-year-old Eskimo boy who feels
assailed by the modernity of his life takes a 1400-mile
journey by dog sled across ice, tundra, and mountains
seeking his own "song" of himself.
1. Eskimos—Juvenile fiction. 2. Children's stories,
American. [1. Eskimos—Fiction] I. Title.
PZ7.P2843Do 1985 [Fic] 84-20443
ISBN 0-689-82165-4

This book is dedicated to
KAY-GWA-DAUSH
to honor her song

CONTENTS

PART ONE

THE
TRANCE

I

I came wet into the world.
 On both sides there were cliffs,
white cliffs that were my mother's thighs.
 And I didn't cry though it was cold
by the white cliffs and I was afraid.
 I came wet into the world.

—an old Eskimo man relating
the memory of his birth in a
snowhouse on the sea ice.

RUSSEL SUSSKIT rolled out of the bunk and put his feet on the floor and listened in the darkness to the sounds of morning.

They were the same sounds he had always heard, sounds he used to listen for. Now in the small government house—sixteen by twenty—they grated like the ends of a broken bone.

He heard his father get up and hack and cough and spit into the stove. His father smoked ciga-

rettes all day, rolled them with Prince Albert tobacco, and had one hanging on his lip late into
the night. In the mornings he had to cough the
cigarettes up. The sound tore at Russel more than
at his father. It meant something that did not
belong on the coast of the sea in a small Eskimo
village. The coughing came from Outside, came
from the tobacco which came from Outside and
Russel hated it.

After the coughing and spitting there was the
sound of the fire being lit, a sound he used to look
forward to as he woke. The rustle of paper and
kindling and diesel fuel, which was used to start
the wood, the scratch of a match, the flame taking
and the stink of the diesel oil filling the one room.
Russel did not like the smell of the diesel oil but
he did not hate it the way he hated his father's
coughing in the morning.

Russell heard the wind outside and that was
good except that it carried the sounds of the village
waking, which meant the sound of snowmachine
engines starting up.

The snowmachines were loud and scared the
seals. To fourteen-year-old Russel the whine of
them above the wind hurt as much as the sound
of coughing. He was coming to hate them, too.

It was still dark in the house because the village

generator hadn't been turned on for the day. The darkness was cut by the light of the oil lamp on the table as his father touched a match to the wick.

Flat light filled the room and Russel looked around as he always did. It was a standard government house—a winter house. They would move to summer fish-camps later. But in the winter they came into the village and stayed in the government houses. Boxes is what they are, really, he thought: boxes to put people in.

In one corner there was a small table with an oilcloth table cover. The cloth was patterned with roses and Russel did not know why his father had ordered it. There were no women there. Russel's mother had been gone for years, gone with a white trapper. But his father had liked the roses on the tablecloth and had sent for it. Russel had never seen a rose except on the tablecloth and on television over at the central meeting house where there was a set for watching. He did not think roses were as pretty as the small flowers that came in the tundra in the summer while they were taking salmon from the rivers. But his father liked the roses and Russel liked his father so he tried liking the roses.

All around the walls were pictures of Jesus.

His father loved Jesus more than he loved the

roses. When he was young his father had told him about Jesus and Russel had listened but he didn't understand. He supposed the idea was something that came when you got old, the understanding of Jesus, and in the meantime he looked at all the pictures and wondered what they meant.

There was one in which Jesus had thorns on his head and they were cutting into him and making him bleed. Russel had asked his father why Jesus would want to do such a thing.

"Because he is the Son of God and is meant to suffer for your sins," his father said, which made no sense at all to Russel: the story of Jesus happened so long ago, back in the Before Time, and Russel couldn't remember doing anything wrong enough to make a man shove thorns in his head. But he said nothing against it. Jesus kept his father from drinking, in some way which he also did not understand, and that was good. When his father used to drink, things were all bad and if Jesus kept that out of his life, even if He did it mysteriously, that was all right.

But he got bored with the pictures around the walls showing Jesus with light in back of him and bleeding and carrying a cross. Even in the tiny bathroom where there was the bucket there was also a picture of Jesus, and another hung over the stove. All the pictures were cut out of religious magazines which people Outside had sent his father.

Two snowmachines went by the house. They were moving fast, too fast to stop in the dark if something jumped out in front of them. Russel winced at the noise.

Russel owned a snowmachine. Owned a motor sled. And he used it. But he didn't like snow-machines and used one only because he needed a means to get around and he didn't have any dogs. There were almost no dogs in the village. Just one team, owned by old Oogruk. And Oogruk didn't use them but simply kept them for memories.

Russel pulled on his felt-duffel slippers and slipped them inside the rubber shoepacs that made up the outer boot. He had slept in his pants and it took only a moment to pull the undershirt on and a sweater.

He stepped out to the food cache in the dark. It was an elevated wooden hut filled with caribou and seal and fish meat. Earlier in the winter the men and boys of the village had gone back into the hills on snowmachines and found a herd of caribou and they had worked around them with rifles, killing into the center. Russel and his father had taken twelve of them, some others had killed twenty or more, and they brought the meat back on sledges pulled by the snowmachines.

Russel used a hatchet to chop off some slivers of caribou and a tiny bit of seal meat. He took them back in the house.

On the wood stove was a pan and he pulled it over onto the heat and threw in the seal and caribou meat. The frozen seal meat started to melt and give off oil immediately and the caribou began to cook in the oil and soon the smell of the meat filled the room and he liked that.

He stood looking down at the pan and when the meat was warm—still nearly raw—he took out a piece of caribou and put it in his mouth and used an *ulu*—a short curved knife—to cut the meat just on the edge of his lips.

He chewed and swallowed, then took another bite. Cutting it cleanly, chewing, staring at the stove, the pan, at nothing.

"You should cook the meat longer," his father said, coming from the bathroom. "We do not eat it raw anymore."

Russel said nothing, nodded, but took more meat.

"There are small things in the meat to make you sick. Small worms and bugs. When you cook the meat more it kills them."

"I was hungry."

"Well. Next time, eh?"

Russel nodded. "Next time."

His father watched the meat cook. "We used to eat everything raw but now we have learned to cook it. That's one of the good things we learned."

Russel smiled. "Raw meat tastes better. You get the blood then."

"That's true. But you also get the small things to make you sick. It's better to cook it."

"Yes, Father." He wanted to go on and say, *Father, I am not happy with myself*, but he did not. It was not the sort of thing you talked about, this feeling he had, unless you could find out what was causing it. He did not know enough of the feeling to talk.

"There were some of the old things that were not bad," his father said. "I am too young to remember many of them, but I was told a lot of them by my father. You did not meet him because before you were born he died in a bad storm on the sea. His *umiak* was torn by ice when they were walrus hunting and all the men in the boat died but one who rode to the ice on a sealskin float. It was an awful thing, an awful thing. The women cut themselves deep and bled in grief when they learned. I was just a small boy, but I remember the grief."

His father scratched himself and took some meat,

still nearly raw. "I like the blood taste, too." He bit, cut and chewed and put the *ulu* back on the stove top.

"Father, something is bothering me."

He replied around the meat. "I know. I have seen it."

"But I don't know what it is."

"I know that, too. It is part that you are fourteen and have thirteen winters and there are things that happen then which are hard to understand. But the other part that is bothering you I cannot say because I lack knowledge. You must get help from some other place."

Russel nodded, then thought. "But where?"

His father looked at the ceiling, back down, thinking. "When I have trouble that I do not understand I sometimes get help from Jesus Christ."

Russel hesitated. He did not want to sound discourteous but he was sure Jesus wouldn't help.

"But you do not have Jesus so that may not work for you. If you do not have Jesus I think you should go and talk to Oogruk. He is old and sometimes wise and he also tells good stories."

"Oogruk? For help?"

His father laughed. "I know. You think he is old and just babbles. But there are two things there, there are Oogruk's words and there is Oogruk's song. Songs and words are not always the same. They do not always say the same thing. Sometimes words lie—but the song is always true. If you listen to Oogruk's words, sometimes they don't make sense. But if you listen to his song, there is much to learn from Oogruk."

"All right. I will go. But will Oogruk give a song to me?"

Russel had heard about the songs his father spoke of. They were private and belonged only to the person who owned them. Now almost no one had a song.

"That is for him to know. Now go and get more meat. You did not bring in enough." His father thought a moment. "And bring in two of the heads so they will begin to thaw."

"You want the heads?"

"Not for me. For Oogruk. Take the heads when you go, as a gift. He loves the eyes."

Russel nodded and went out into the dark again.

2

There was a time when I was young. It was a
bad time when there was not meat anywhere you
looked and we had eaten of all the dogs.

We asked our old mother if we could kill her
and eat of her until the deer came back and we
would have done that thing. We would have
done that thing. But that morning a deer came
and my uncle took it with an arrow in the right
manner and we did not have to do that thing.
More deer came and we did not have to eat
our old mother.

—an old Eskimo telling of his youth.

RUSSEL HAD been in Oog-
ruk's house many times but he always stopped
before he went in. The dogs always drew him,
drew his eyes over and he stopped. They were
tied near the elevated food cache—a rough log hut
up on stilts—and they watched him with inter-
ested eyes, slanted, deep eyes, watched him as he
threw the caribou heads on the ledge surrounding
the food cache.

The dogs.

There were five of them. Great red beasts with blue eyes, a cross between wolf and Mackenzie River huskies with some Coppermine River village blood mixed in. They were shy, aloof dogs who did not want people to touch them except to harness them or feed them. Russel knew little of dogs, but a man who knew dogs said they were good.

They were the only team in the village and never worked, so they were fat. But the fat hid muscle that could go forever.

Russel turned away from them and went to the door of Oogruk's house. Again he stopped, hesitating. It wasn't that he was afraid to go in. Everybody was welcome at Oogruk's. The old man loved company. It was more that Oogruk lived differently and inside the house—which outside looked like any government box—you had to change. The mind had to change, and the nose—Russel thought, grimacing—because Oogruk lived the old way. He would not allow electricity, used a seal-oil lamp and had skins on the floor. Some of the skins, all from caribou, were green tanned and they smelled when they grew warm. It was not a bad smell but it was strong and took some getting used to.

As did Oogruk. The way of Oogruk, the way he looked and was; it took a different thinking.

Russel opened the door without knocking, as

was the custom, and went in and closed the door. Outside there had been bright-light and sea-wind off the frozen sea ice, salt-wind. Inside it was almost pitch-dark. The windows were covered with smoke grime, and the room was full of smoke from the lamp on a box in the corner, a seal-oil lamp with a moss wick that threw a tiny yellow glow around the room.

Leaning against the wall were harpoons and lances, hanging on nails were arrow-bags and bows and small ivory carvings. On other nails were skin clothes, squirrel-skin undergarments and caribou-skin parkas, some old and some not so old, all hanging loosely and thick with the smoke.

Against the far wall sat Oogruk. At first it was hard to know where the smoke ended and Oogruk began. Except for a small breechclout he was nude, and his skin was the same color as the smoke, a tan-brown, rich and oily. His hair had gone white, or would have been white, but it had taken the smoke, too, seemed to have flown into the smoke and become part of the smoke from the lamp.

"Hello. Hello. You sit down and we'll talk for a while." The voice was strong—it always amazed Russel to hear Oogruk's voice. He was so old but the voice moved like strong music. "I will talk for you."

Russel nodded and sat near the right wall, glad

that nobody else was there. Often children would come in to listen—with respect, but out of curiosity more than anything—and Russel was glad that they were not there now. "I brought some deer heads for you," he said when he'd settled on the hides. "With the eyes. They are out on the platform."

Oogruk swiveled his head to face Russel. The eyes were opaque, a milk blindness over them, but Russel never thought of him as blind.

"I eat of the eyes when I can but people don't save them anymore," Oogruk said.

"Should I bring them in?"

"Later. Later. Did you see my dogs when you came in?"

Russel nodded, then remembered the blindness and said aloud, "Yes. They are well. They are fat."

"Good. I don't drive them anymore but they are good dogs and I worry that they don't get fed enough."

"They are being taken care of by everybody—they are all right."

Oogruk said nothing for a time. The eyes moved back to the flame from the lamp so the thick-white caught the yellow of the light and glowed for a second.

"Dogs are like white people," Oogruk said,

looking at the flame. "They do not know how to get a settled mind. They are always turning, looking for a better way to lie down. And if things go wrong they have anger and frustration. They are not like us. It is said that dogs and white people come from the same place." He snorted—a nasal sound, a kind of *chaa* sound through his nose that could have meant anything from scorn to anger to humor. "I do not know how true that is because white people are clearly not dogs. But they have many of the same ways and so one wonders."

Russel nodded but said nothing. One time he had seen a bushpilot who had crashed his plane near the village. The plane was broken in the middle and the pilot had stood screaming at it and kicking it for failing him and falling from the sky. He treated the plane like a living animal until he got tired, then he walked away as a dog would walk away from a stick he'd been tearing at.

Oogruk sighed. "I will tell you about something. We used to have songs for everything, and nobody knows the songs anymore. There were songs for dogs, for good dogs or bad dogs, and songs to make them work or track bear. There were songs for all of everything. I used to know a song that would make the deer come to me so that I could kill it. And I knew a man who could sing a song for whales and make them come to his harpoon."

The flame guttered in the lamp and Russel saw Oogruk use a small ivory tool to brush the burned moss away to clean the flame. A new-yellow filled the room, cut through the smoke, then paled down as the twisted moss burned on the end.

Russel shifted and stuck his legs out straight in front of him—Eskimo fashion—and relaxed. He leaned back against the wall. There were things he wanted to ask but he did not know what they were. Part of his mind was turning over, but another part was full of a strange patience and so he waited. Sometimes it was better to wait.

"Mebbe you could bring in those eyes and put some snow in the pot and we'll warm them up. Cold eyes are bad to eat."

Russel got up and went outside. The wind was stronger now, bringing cold off the ice, but he didn't wear a coat and liked the tightness the cold caused when it worked inside his light shirt. He used his belt knife to pop the caribou eyes out of the two skulls—they levered out with surprising difficulty—and stopped by the door to take down the pan hanging on the wall and fill it with snow.

He put the eyes on top and took the pan and

snow inside and handed them to Oogruk, who held the pan over the lamp.

"One misses women," the old man said. "I had some good wives but they are gone. Two died back before the white men came, died bearing children, and the last one just left. She went up to the mining town to a party and didn't come back. One misses women."

Russel said nothing. He was seated again, leaning against the wall, and as with dogs he knew nothing of women. The girls smiled at him with round faces and merry eyes but he was not ready for women yet and so knew nothing of them.

"They cooked and sewed for me. Eyes and meat taste better when cooked by women. That's the truth."

Russel had never eaten eyes. He knew the fluid in them would be too salty. He smiled. "Were there songs for the women, too?" He wanted Oogruk to talk of the songs again.

Oogruk grinned, the teeth worn down to the gums, the hair hanging down past his cheeks. As the memory grew so did the grin until finally, after a couple of minutes, he laughed openly. "They always shined in the snow houses, shined with fat and oil. It was a thing to be young then—it was everything to be young then. It wasn't that there were songs for women," he said, coming back to the subject, "it's that the women *were* the songs."

Russel reached over. The pot was tipping in Oogruk's hand and the melted snow was about to spill into the lamp and douse the flame.

Oogruk stuck a finger in the water and found it to be warm. He reached into the pan and took out an eye and popped it in his mouth, using his gums to crush it and swallow the juice noisily.

"Have one." He held the pan out. "They are good."

"I brought them for you. Besides, I ate before I left our house. I had meat."

Oogruk nodded and slowly, one by one, ate the other three eyes, smacking his lips with the joy of it. When he was done he slapped his stomach. "They are good. Later, when you are gone for the long time, you will wish you had eaten of them."

Russel almost missed it. Then it hit him. "What do you mean, 'gone for the long time'?"

But Oogruk was again in his memories. "I saw a thing once that was hard to understand. We were talking of songs and this man lived when I was young and he was very old and he had a song for the small birds. They would fly in flocks that moved this way and that and would flick the light of the sun off their breasts. Snowbirds. So this man was named Ulgavik and he had a song to make the birds dance. When he sang it one way they would fly that way and when he wanted them to change he would sing it another way and they would take the light and go the new way.

"It was a thing of beauty."

But Russel was fixed on the earlier comment.

"What did you mean about being gone for the long time?"

"This man Ulgavik knew dogs. He knew birds, but he knew dogs, too, so that when he got old and his eyes went to milk it did not matter. He could run his team blind and knew the dogs so well that what the dogs saw came back up through the sled and he saw that, too. The dogs were his eyes. Maybe if Ulgavik were alive he would tell you how to know dogs and birds."

Russel closed his eyes and thought of Ulgavik running blind out across the sea ice, blind into the white—but such a thing couldn't be.

"What we need is some *muktuk*," Oogruk said. "I haven't had any for a long time. Do you know where there is some *muktuk*?"

"No. Everybody is out of it." Russel thought of the delicate little squares of whale blubber that had been fermented all summer in rancid seal oil. They had a nutty, sweet-stink taste. But the village had not taken a whale that year, which was considered very bad luck. Russel thought it was because of the snowmachines, because they scared the seals and whales away by sending their ugly noise down through the ice. But he didn't say what he thought. "There will be no whales until the ice is gone and then I don't think they will come."

Oogruk was quiet for a time. Then he sighed. "Because of the machines."

Russel started. "Is that what you think?"

"No. That is what you think. I think they will not come because we are wrong now and don't deserve them and they know that. We don't have the songs anymore and they don't hear us singing and so they know we don't deserve *muktuk*. Of course I could be wrong and it could be the machines."

"How did you know I felt that way about the snowmachines?"

Again the flame sputtered and again Oogruk trimmed it to bring the light up and Russel only then realized with a start that if Oogruk was blind, truly blind, he could not see the flame sputter.

"It is the way one thinks," Oogruk said. "I know the way you think and so I know what you feel about the machines and the whales."

"How can you tell when the lamp goes down if you can't see?" Russel blurted.

"Questions. Questions. Did you come here to

ask questions or did you come here to find the way it was?"

And Russel knew he was right. In truth he had not known why he came to Oogruk's house, just that he had to come, that something had been bothering him. Just as his father had known that something had been bothering him, and that Jesus probably wouldn't be able to help him, even though he helped Russel's father quit drinking.

But Oogruk was right. That's why he had come. There was something wrong with the way things were now, something wrong with him. He wanted to be more, somehow, but when he looked ahead he didn't see more, he saw only less.

Oogruk wiped his face with his hands and smoothed the shine of the oil and sweat. He turned to face Russel and his voice grew serious. "Some of my memory is like my eyes, dead and gone. That is the way of age. And so some of the things I should tell you I can't, because they are gone. Just gone. Like melted ice in the spring. I held them as long as I could but many of them are gone now."

"That is all right. Tell me what you can and that will be enough."

"I don't know. I don't know if it will be enough for what you have to do. But it is all I have. Still, one is hungry."

Russel thought of the food cache outside. "Is there meat in your cache? I could bring some in."

Oogruk nodded. "There is much meat. Deer and a seal that some young men brought by. Why don't you bring in a piece of the deer and we'll put it in the pot and get it warm? Maybe the warm meat will help my memory."

Russel went outside and opened the cache. There was no seal but there were some parts of caribou, two back legs and eight or nine front shoulders. Oogruk obviously couldn't hunt for himself and so people brought him spare meat. That explained all the front shoulders—it was not the best part of the animal. The tenderloin down the back was gone—the best part—so Russel took one of the back legs out. He used an ax leaning on the shelf to cut off large slivers, long chunks, of the marbled meat, happy to see the fat streaks and thick layer of fat on the legs.

Fat was everything. And while deer fat wasn't as good as whale or seal or even pig lard from the trading post, it was good enough when it was hot. It turned to tallow on the lips when it cooled, but at first it was all right.

Some of the chips from the ax flew into the nearest dog's circle and he got up slowly and walked out on his chain to pick them up.

"Lazy dog," Russel said aloud and was answered by a low growl. Not one of anger but of shyness and suspicion—a low rumble that came from the dog's chest.

Russel didn't know the dog's name, didn't know any of the dogs. Always they were just Oogruk's dogs; it was Oogruk's dogs making noise howling, or Oogruk's dogs who had bitten somebody, or Oogruk's dogs who had gotten into a fight. He didn't know their names.

With the meat under one arm like large red pages from a thick book he went back into the house. It was still light, hazy light, but the light only held for three hours a day. He knew it would be dark soon. Across the ice would come the late afternoon wind and light, both hitting the village, the light dying as it always did in the winter, dropping fast, and the wind making huge drifts off the beach. Sometimes, in the late middle of the winter, the drifts became so large they covered the houses.

Inside he put a couple of slivers of meat in the pot and Oogruk held it over the lamp to warm it up.

Another question was bothering Russel, one inspired by the dogs and he decided to ask it. "You have dogs but there is no sled. Don't you have a sled?"

Oogruk nodded. "In the lean-to next to the house. It is old but made of hardwood that came from the sea and so has strength."

When the deer meat was heating on the lamp—Oogruk holding it over the flame with a corded arm, a wire arm—the old man let breath out of his nose.

"I have not been counting the summers and winters of my age," he said. "But I am old. I am old enough that I hunted before we had guns, old enough to remember what it was like before."

Russel was once again seated, legs sticking out straight, leaning back against the wall. The smell of the heating deer meat mixed with the smell of the smoke from the lamp and made him hungry. The smoke smelled like burned meat, the salty smell of burned meat. "It must have been something back then."

Oogruk made the *chaa* sound. "It was more than that. We lived so differently, so far back and different that it almost cannot be understood now. Now they use guns and make noise, back then we were quiet and the animals felt different about dying. But that's just one thing, one little thing that was different."

A third time Russel got up. He went to the wall where the weapons hung and took down a small bow, made of wood laminated with slivers of horn, wrapped with rawhide. It had a string made of sinew and after much grunting and heaving he got the bow strung. When he tried to pull it back his shoulders knotted but the string only came back four or five inches.

All this while Oogruk sat quietly, waiting, an air of study on his face.

Russel unstrung the bow and put it back on the wall. There was a skin pouch of arrows that he took down and he pulled several arrows out of it. They had bone and antler points, some with jagged barbs, others with smooth edges.

"There is a museum in the mining town," Russel said. "I was there once when I was sick and went up to the doctor. In the museum are many things like this bow and those lances. Some of them from back a long time."

Oogruk nodded. "I have not been up to the town, though I have had many chances. But I have heard of the museum and the old tools. There is a difference. I have used these weapons to take meat. They do not belong in a museum," he snorted, "any more than I belong in a museum. These tools are for using, not looking at."

Russel took down a lance. The shaft was of wood that had been scraped and straightened to take the ivory cup and point on the end. The point itself was a small toggle, razor sharp, that would tip once it entered the animal and be impossible to pull out. The toggle point was attached to a piece of supple leather, a long lashing, that had been kept soft and greased. Just as the bow and arrows had been kept in good shape.

"All these years," Russel said. "All this time you have taken care of these things."

"When I was a young man I came down this coast in a *umiak* with four other men. We had some trouble back in a village up north and we came down to make this village. After we found meat we went to get wives and we made this place where we are now."

"You made this village?"

"At first just us. Then others came because there were good fish here and much game. And so it was a good place and we had good food and good songs. Everybody had a song then and that song was just for that person. That's how it was."

"What happened to the songs? Why don't we have them anymore?"

Oogruk set the pot down and rested his arm. The meat was still too cold to eat. He picked the pot up and held it over the flame again, using the small tool to clean the moss wick first. "We had those songs until the first missionary came. He said they were wrong for some reason or another, like dancing was wrong. At first nobody believed him and we laughed at him. But he kept talking about it being wrong to have the songs and the dances and said how we would go to hell if we did not give them up. Of course we laughed again because we did not understand what this hell was . . ."

He took a breath. Russel knew about hell from his father, the same way he knew about Jesus.

"It was not that we were stupid," Oogruk continued. "Just that we didn't know about hell. So he told us. About fire and pain and these demons—as he called them—who would tear the strips of meat off us. So, many of the people quit singing and dancing because they feared hell. And even when the missionary became crazy with the winter and we had to drive him out the damage was done. People were afraid to sing and dance and we lost our songs."

Russel frowned. "Can we get them back? Could I get a song?"

Oogruk thought for a time. "It is not like that. You don't get songs, you *are* a song. When we gave up our songs because we feared hell we gave up our insides as well. If we lived the way we used to live, mebbe the songs would come back. Mebbe if we lived the right way again." His voice took on a sadness and became soft. "But nobody is doing that."

"I will."

It came without Russel knowing it was coming. A simple statement. Two words. And when he said them he knew he meant them. He needed to go back and become a song.

"I will," he repeated, leaning once more against the wall. "I will try to get a song. No. I *will* get a song, I will be a song. But I don't know what to do. I don't know how to do it."

Oogruk nodded. "That is true. There has been nobody to teach you. All the fathers have moved from the old ways and so have the mothers and so the long time required to pass on the right information is not there." Oogruk fell into silence.

"If you wanted to," Russel prompted, "you could tell me the way."

At length Oogruk nodded again. "That is why you are here, of course. You are here to learn. And I will try. I will try. But I do not know it all and there will be things I miss. Still, we will do what we can."

All this time he had been holding the meat pot over the fire and now he set it aside. The meat was steaming and he took a piece out and produced an *ulu* and bit down and cut and chewed with worn gums, swallowing when the meat was softened. Russel took some meat and tore with his teeth—he had no knife with him—and chewed and swallowed and they made no talk while they ate.

There was some fat on the meat and the grease ran down their chins and hardened and Russel used his arm to wipe it away.

They ate until the meat was gone. And when they were done with the meat Oogruk picked up the pot and drank deeply and handed it to Russel, who did the same. The water-blood soup was still warm and went down easily.

The silence grew when they'd finished eating but it was not wrong. Russel felt like sleeping yet when he closed his eyes it wasn't sleep that came. It was more a trance, a gentle lowering of his thoughts until he was relaxed, his belly full of warm meat and juice, his mouth full of the taste of the deer meat.

And while he was so, his mind warm and down, the wind tearing through the darkness around the house, bringing snow off the ice to make the big drifts, covering the dogs and the garbage of the village; while he was down, down and back, Oogruk started to talk.

3

*I was round and had great beauty. For that
reason I had no trouble getting husbands and
that was good because they all died. I had three
husbands and they all died before I had twenty
summers. The sea took two of them when their
kayaks were ripped and a great bear took the
third. All I found was his head on the ice. It
was hard then but not bad although I missed my
husbands for a time. But I got a new one and he
lasted.*

—Eskimo woman relating her youth.

NORTH AND EAST of the
village the land rose away from the sea in rolling
hills that led to mountains. Even in the middle of
the winter the land fought to hold the snow. The
short tundra grass gave no foothold and so often
the surface was blown free of snow and the grass
was out all winter.

Arctic hares fed in the bare areas, as did ptarmigan, the small white grouselike birds sometimes

flocking two and three hundred birds in a single place. Now and then, even in the dark-cold of winter, it was possible to see a frozen blue or purple flower—winter flowers.

Russel sat on the edge of the sled and looked down at one such flower by his foot. It had four petals, and he did not understand how it could have gotten through the fall and into the middle of winter. But it had. And it had grown in beauty for it, the color rich against the cold brown of the grass.

Much had changed.

Oogruk had talked until he was done and when he was done he had fallen silent. It might have taken days and nights, it felt like years, and when he was finished Russel had fallen asleep, a real sleep this time. He slept without moving, leaning against the wall and when he awakened the room was cool—still not cold—and he got up stiffly and stretched.

Oogruk was silent, with his eyes closed, the lamp burned out. For a moment Russel thought he was dead, but he was still breathing and Russel took a deerskin and wrapped it around the old man's shoulders.

He knew what to do. From the walls he took the lances and bow and arrows. He also took a pair of bearskin pants and the squirrel underparka and the deerskin outerparka with the hair on the inside. Some of the hair was brittle on the deerskin but it was still thick and warm.

He did not think of the objects as belonging to him, just thought of them as being what he needed. Oogruk had told him to use what he needed, including the dogs and sled and Russel followed those thoughts as if they had been his own, as in some way they were.

He was wearing store pants and a coat and he took them off and hung them on the pegs. For a moment he stood naked in the cooling room, felt his skin tighten. Then he pulled on the bearskin pants, with the hair out, the skin soft and supple. Oogruk had worked oil into the leather to maintain them as he had taken care of everything. At the top there was a drawcord and he pulled it tight. The pants were just slightly large, but the right length.

On the wall were sealskin mukluks. He took them down and felt inside. The grass bottoms were still good and he pulled them on, tied them up around his calves over the bearskin.

Then came the squirrelskin innerparka with the hair out, soft and fine, like leather silk. Last he pulled over the outerparka, thick deerhide, with the hair in, and when that was on and shrugged in place he took down a pair of deer-hide mittens with a shoulder thong and pulled them on.

As soon as he was dressed he went outside before he could heat up. He had to get the sled out of the lean-to on the side of the house and see how much work it needed. The harnesses were also there and the gangline.

It was cold, standing cold. So cold you could spit and it would bounce. When the wind hit him he pulled up the hood and tightened the drawstring through the wolverine ruff. The long fur came in around his face and stopped the wind. Then he pulled up the mitten cuffs and felt the air movement through the parka stop. His body brought the temperature up almost immediately.

Around the sea side of the house Oogruk or somebody had made a lean-to. The door had leather hinges and a wooden pin through the latch. Russel pulled the pin and worked the door open against the snow.

Inside stood a dogsled and there were harnesses on a peg on the wall. He reached in and pulled the sled out to examine it more closely. The sky was light now, a gray all-around haze off the sea and out of the clouds at the same time, and he thought he'd never seen anything so beautiful as the sled in the gray light.

It was the old kind of sled, the kind they called basket sleds. When the modern, white mushers ran the races, they used toboggans made with plastic and bolted together. Ugly little tough sleds.

But in the old days the people used sleds of delicate hardwood lashed with rawhide, all flexible and curved gracefully. Oogruk's was like a carving of a sled, with birch rails down the side and elegant curved stanchions. Around the front was a warped-wood brushbow—something he'd never need unless he ran where there were trees—and it had one-eighth-inch brass runner shoes that looked almost new.

There was a steel snowhook tied to the bridle and a rope gangline with tugs and neck-lines already in place.

He spread it out on the snow and studied everything carefully. The lashing on the sled looked old, but had been oiled and was in good shape. The rope on the gangline was a corded nylon and looked also to be in top condition.

He pulled the harnesses down and spread them out and went over them carefully as well. They were clean, had been patched a few times but were good for all of that.

All he needed was a dog team.

The harnesses all seemed the same size so he put them on the tugs, using the small ivory toggles to tie them in. Then he set the snowhook and pulled the gangline out in front of the sled and stopped to see what he had.

He had never run a team himself. But he'd seen mushers go by in races—one long-distance race went by the village—and he knew how things should look.

He took the lead dog off the chain. It growled at him and raised its hair but he tightened his grip and paid no attention to the snarl. The dog held back and Russel had to drag him to the gangline. The dogs had run for Oogruk but that was more than two years earlier. They had not run since for anybody. And this stranger had to earn their respect, earn the run. The leader turned his shoulder in the curve that meant threat, the curve that meant attack, and lifted his lip to Russel. It was an open challenge and Russel cuffed him across the head with a stiff hand. Still the dog growled and now took a cut at Russel's leg and Russel hit the dog harder.

Then a thing happened, a thing from the trance with Oogruk, and he leaned down so his head was over the top of the leader's head and he growled down at the dog. He did not know why he did this, did not know for certain what the growl meant but when it was finished he curved his head over the dog's head and, still without knowing for sure why, he bit down, hard, across the bridge of the dog's nose.

The leader growled and flashed teeth but quickly backed down and that was the end of it. He stood to in harness, pulling the gangline out tight while Russel turned to bring the rest of the team.

The other four dogs came nicely and settled into harness as if they'd been working all along. Russel smiled. It almost looked like a dog team.

He had in mind this first time to just take the dogs out on the ice and see what happened. He took no weapons or other gear because he wasn't sure if he could control the team and didn't want to lose anything if the sled flipped.

The first run was rough. The dogs ran as a gaggle, wide open, in a tangled bunch and not lined out as they should have been. Russel ran into them with the sled more than once when they stopped—before he could get the brake on—and when they hit the so-called pressure ridges a mile offshore, where the ice from the sea ground against the shore ice and piled up, he almost lost the sled.

They tipped him and dragged him on his face

for a quarter of a mile before he could get the snowhook set in a crack.

When he had stopped them he put the sled upright and sat on it for a moment to think. It was close to dark, the quick three-hour day all but gone, and he would have to head back to the village, yet he did not want to leave the run.

The wind cut at his cheeks and he turned his hood away from the force, took the cold.

"You will have to know me," he said quietly to the dogs after a time. "Just as I will have to know you."

Two of them looked back at him. It was perhaps not an invitation. It was perhaps not a look that meant anything at all except that they looked back and their eyes caught his eyes and he knew they would run. He *knew* they would run. He knew when he put his feet to the sled and took the handlebar in his hands that they would run and he did not know how he knew this but only that it was so.

When he was on the runners he reached down and disengaged the snowhook and used the small lip-squeak sound that Oogruk had told him to use to get the dogs running.

They were off so fast he was almost jerked backward off the sled. It wasn't a gaggle now, but a pulling force with all the dogs coordinating to line the sled out across the ice, a silent curve of power out ahead of him.

The feeling, he thought, the feeling is that the sled is alive; that I am alive and the sled is alive and the snow is alive and the ice is alive and we are all part of the same life.

He did not try to steer them that first time and they ran up the coast on the ice for three or four miles before their fat caught up with them and they slowed. When they were down to a trot, tongues slavering off the heat from their run, Russel stopped them again.

Oogruk said the leader had been gee-haw trained the same as the white freighters did—to go right on gee, left on haw.

"Gee!" Russel made it a loud command but he needn't have. The lead dog turned off to the right and started out again, back in toward shore. When they got along the beach edge, where the ice was mixed with sand, Russel turned right again and headed back for the village.

The dogs automatically headed for Oogruk's house and their chains, and Russel let them go. When they pulled in he took them out of harness and put them back on the chains and went into the house.

Oogruk was awake and sitting by the lamp. He had moved, Russel could tell by his position, but he was back and he smiled when Russel came in.

"Did they run for you?" the old man asked. "Did they run for you?"

Russel shrugged out of the parkas, down to bare skin. He laughed. "They ran, Grandfather. They ran for me like the wind."

"Ahh. That is fine, that is fine."

"It was a feeling, a feeling like being alive. The sled flew across the ice and I was alive with the sled."

"Yes. Yes. That is so—this is how it should be. You are correct."

"Is there meat left? We should eat meat."

The old man laughed. "You are a true person. Eat when you are happy. No. We ate it all last time. Get more from the cache. But first feed the dogs. Give them meat three times bigger than your fist. Always take care of the dogs first."

The words were not meant as a rebuke but they made Russel stop and think that perhaps he had been inconsiderate. He pulled on the light inner-parka and went outside. It took him a few minutes to chop meat for the dogs and to get some for themselves and when he got back in the cabin Oogruk had the pot on the flame waiting. He had already put snow in the pot to melt and Russel was mystified as to how the old blind man could have gotten out and found snow and gotten back in to sit without Russel seeing him.

Russel put the deer pieces in the pot and took his position on the floor. He had, essentially, moved in with the old man. Not that it was strange. In the normal Eskimo culture people moved around on a whim, especially young people. It was as natural as calling old people grandparents whether they were actually related or not.

"This is good meat," Oogruk said as the deer cooked. "But we need fresh. Fresh meat. You will have to hunt for us."

Russel nodded. "I was thinking the same thing. But what should I hunt?"

Oogruk snorted. "Whatever there is. But maybe you should start small. Go out after we eat and sleep and try to get some hare or ptarmigan."

And they had eaten, and slept, and Russel had the team out in the hills to hunt fresh meat for the old man: for himself and the old man.

He was hunting with the bow and had had many shots at both hares and ptarmigan but hadn't hit any yet. The arrows wouldn't fly true, wouldn't go where he wanted them to go. Always they were just under or over or left or right—just enough to miss. On one ptarmigan he shot six times with the round-headed bird arrows and the bird just sat as the arrows *shusshed* past. Finally he flew.

Russel looked at the dogs. They were all down, but not out of tiredness as much as boredom. The country has nothing for them to see, he thought; it is my mind that is wrong. Not the bow. It is my mind.

"What should I do?" he asked. "What is it that I am doing wrong?"

He closed his eyes and when they were shut the answer came to him. Oogruk had told him during his trance, had told him how to use the lances and the bow.

"Look to the center of the center of where the point will go. Look *inside* the center," the old man had said.

And so he pulled the hook and squeaked the team up and ran a few miles over the rolling hills until the team scared up another flock of ptarmigan. This time the dogs saw them and heard them and he had a good ride until he could get them stopped as they chased the birds. When he finally got them down he set the hook and took the bow off the sled.

The quiver he put over one shoulder but he kept out two of the bird arrows and put one of them in the bow.

The birds had flown over a small ridge and he followed, walking slowly, keeping his head down as he approached the top of the ridge.

Most of them had gone across. But eight or ten had landed just past the high point and two of them were hunkered under a small piece of willow, nearly hidden white-against-white.

Russel drew the bow, but Oogruk's advice stopped him. He looked at the nearest bird more closely. Rather than just see the bird he tried to find the exact spot he wanted the arrow to hit. Then he tried to see in the center of that tiny spot and he drew and released the bowstring and the arrow moved across the space, floated across and took the bird in a shower of feathers, and the commotion frightened the other birds away in a cloud of flying white streaks.

Russel ran over to the bird and picked it up. He had killed many ptarmigan with the small rifle that spit—the .22—but never one in the old way, with the bow.

"When you kill the old way," Oogruk had said, "it is because the animal wishes to be taken then. You must thank the animal by leaving the head with food in the mouth—if it's a land animal. With sea animals, you put fresh water in their mouths."

He pulled off the head and found some dried berries on a branch and put them in the bird's beak and put the head under the bush. "Thank you for this good meat," he said. "It will be enjoyed."

A part of him felt silly for that. He was far enough away from the old way still to almost not believe in it. Yet another part of him felt right, more right than he'd been in a long time.

It was coming dark as he trudged back to the sled. The dogs were sitting up as he came toward them and they wagged their tails when they saw the bird.

"Some meat," he said to them. "Not much but a start. A start."

He put the bird in the sled bag and tied the bow and quiver back on the sled, pulled the hook and called the dogs up.

He did not want to go back to the village yet. Even if it was too dark to hunt more he could run out along the tundra and see the country. There was no trail and he let the dogs have their heads, or let the leader run. The rest followed wherever he went.

Russel stood easily on the runners and held the

handlebar loosely. When he'd first run the dogs he was tight and rigid—afraid of losing them—but he was quickly coming to realize the sled had a life of its own. It was very flexible, giving and taking the bumps with a flowing motion, and it made gentle sounds. The rawhide lashing points creaked softly and the runners hummed, a kind of high-pitched *sssss* sound that was very pleasant to the ear. Riding was more a matter of fitting in to the sled than trying to control it. With his knees relaxed and his hips loose he could shift his weight only slightly and the sled turned with him. It became almost an extension of his body, just as he was becoming almost an extension of the dogs.

They started down a long slope, across at an angle, perhaps a mile of downhill running, and the snow was packed so they didn't sink in. In seconds they were running wide open, their tongues flying, their ears laid flat, tails down.

Russel kept one foot on the claw brake to keep the sled from running up on them and a great joy grew within him.

The silence was broken by his laugh but the dogs didn't look back. They drove on down the hill, the sled flying from hummock to hummock, Russel laughing and playing the sled back and forth to miss the larger mounds. Twice it flipped on its side but he stayed with it and it bounced back onto its runners, all the time careening down the hill.

When they finally reached the bottom he stopped the team and set the hook.

It was then he saw the caribou. She was standing, side to him, part of the gathering darkness, part of all he could see. She had a ghost quality, the light fur of her belly blending with the snow color. He held his breath.

Hold for me, he thought, hold for me, deer. He moved slowly and took the bow from the case. It was still strung from when he was hunting the ptarmigan and he took out one of the wide-ivory-tipped big-headed arrows and fitted it to the bow.

Inside the center of the center of the caribou, he thought—that's where the arrow must fly.

Still she stood. Waiting, looking at him and the dogs, and he pulled the bow and released it and did not see it fly in the dusk but he knew, he *knew* that it flew as his mind would have it fly.

The caribou hunched slightly at the shoulder and took four steps and folded down, the front legs bending slowly, almost as if she were going to sleep. The dogs had held silently but when they saw her hit and going down it triggered the prey response from the wolf memory and they went mad. They slammed against the harnesses, again and again until the hook jerked out of the snow and the sled came loose and the team was on the deer in a tangled mass, some tearing at her throat, some at her back legs, some at her belly.

Russel ran after them. Using the bow as a club, yelling and hitting and throwing them back, he finally got them under control and off the dying caribou. It took five more minutes to get them lined out in the opposite direction from the animal and when he turned back the deer was dead.

He stopped and looked down at her. The feathers of the arrow protruded from just in back of the shoulder. The arrow had gone through the heart. She had died with her head to the east, which was good, and Russel found some of the sweet tundra grass the caribou liked and put it in her mouth. When the ritual was done he stood away from her and looked above the deer's head and said: "Thank you for this meat, deer. It will be enjoyed."

From the sled back he took the short knife he'd gotten from Oogruk and made the gut cut, from the ribs back, and dropped the large stomach. He reached in for the liver and heart and cut them out and set them aside for Oogruk. The old man could get the eyes later. Reaching up and in he jerked the lungs out and cut them in five pieces and gave them to the dogs, only just keeping his hands safe from their lunging, again using the bow as a club to stop their fighting. The blood smell was strong for them and they wanted to fight.

"Ha!" He snorted. "We are tough now, are we? When we smell the hot guts we are all tough."

The deer was heavy and he had to work hard to get her carcass loaded on the sled. When he had her on and tied in he put the liver and heart back in the open cavity, washed his hands in the snow and put mittens back on. As long as he'd been working on the deer her body heat had kept him warm, but he now realized that it was getting very cold and his hands had lost function in moments. They hurt as the mitts warmed them and he smiled with the cold-pain. He thought of cold not as an enemy but as many different kinds of friend, or a complicated ally.

Cold brought the first ice to the sea, the first strong ice so they could get out and hunt seals. Cold brought the fattening up of game so it was good to eat. It brought snow and made everything clean, it made storing meat and fish easy.

Cold could kill as well. But if treated fairly, if treated as a friend and if caution was taken, cold was good.

Russel's fingers took pain for a time from his friend the cold and he smiled with it, smiled with the deer on the sled and the cold and the dogs: the dogs out in front, coming around in a large curve, heading back for the village with the deer and the ptarmigan, the dogs moving in the dark silently with the hot lungs in their bellies and the joy on them from the kill, the dogs with their shoulders curving over and down with the weight of the deer and Russel pulling back against them as they fought up the hill, fought up with lunges and heaves to pull the sled over, over at last onto the crown of the ridge.

In the distance he could see the lights of the village from the ridge height. It was about ten miles away, but the night was clear and cold now, and almost still. The wind was dying off with the cold and darkness.

Knowing they would spend another night in their kennel the dogs picked up the speed, even with the weight of the deer, until they were moving in a steady easy lope that would cover the distance to the village in thirty minutes.

Russel was full of the night and the dogs as they ran and he felt himself go out to the dogs, out ahead. At first he didn't understand it, couldn't define it enough to give it form. But in moments the feeling grew and in his mind he gave it words, moving words, dog words.

Out before me they go
taking me home.
Out before me they go
I am the dogs.

He realized that it was part of a song, moving through the dark toward the village lights.

He wondered if it was part of his song and decided that it might be. He would make it grow.

Tonight in the village he would let it be known that he was a new person, not the old Russel, and he would tell the story to Oogruk and anybody who would listen, the story of how he took the deer with the arrow that flew across the dark.

And the telling would become part of the song.

4

Those white men came a long time ago. The
white men who talked with rocks in their
mouths. They came and took and took it all.
They used our men as beasts and they took our
women for their own and left us with no meat.
Left us starving. They took all the fur and then
they left. That is what I was told when I was
young and in those villages they still don't like
the white men who talk with rocks in their
mouth.

—Eskimo speaking about the early Russian
fur hunters who came for pelts.

SEA ICE IS not the same as
fresh-water ice. The salt-water ice is stronger, more
elastic, isn't as slippery. Also the sea ice moves
all the time, even when it is thick. Sometimes
whole cakes of the ice will go out to sea, miles
across, sliding out to sea and taking anybody on
the cake with it.

On the fourth day after taking the deer with
the arrow Russel took the team out on the ice to

find seals. Oogruk wanted oil for the lamp and he wanted some seal meat and fat to eat and he said these things in such a way that Russel felt it would be good to find a seal to take with the harpoon. It wasn't that he actually asked, or told Russel to go for seal, but he talked about how it was to hunt in the old days.

"Out on the edge of the ice, where it meets the sea but well back from the edge, sometimes there are seal holes. The seals come up through them and sit on the ice and if you are there when they come you can get the small harpoon point in them. That is the way it was done. Men would leave their dogs well back and pile a mound of snow in front of them and wait for the seal. Wait and wait." Oogruk had scratched with his nails on the wall of the house. "When the seal starts to come there is a scratching sound and the hunter must be ready to put the point in then."

"How long must one wait?" Russel asked.

"There is not a time. Waiting for seals is not something you measure. You get a seal, that is all. Some men go a whole winter and get none, some will get one right away. Hunting seals with the small point and the killing lance is part of the way to live."

So Russel went out on the ice. He took the team away in the daylight and was twenty miles out, working heavily through pressure ridges, when the storm came off the sea.

He had seen many storms. In his years with the village, every winter brought violent storms off the sea, white walls of wind and driven snow. Twice he had been caught out on a snowmachine and had to run for the village ahead of the wall coming across the ice.

But with a dog team you did not run ahead of the wall. As he was crossing a pressure ridge, pushing the dogs up and over the broken, jagged edges, he heaved up on the sled and looked out across the ice, out to sea, and a great boiling wall of white was rising to the sky. In seconds it was impossible to tell where the sky ended and the sea ice began and Russel knew he would have to hide before it hit. He fought the sled down the pressure ridge and brought the dogs around into a small hole under an overlapping ice ledge. There was barely room to pull his legs in.

He tipped the sled over to make a rough door across the opening to block the wind and pulled the dogs in on top of him. Working as fast as he could he tried to pack snow into the slats of the sled bottom but before he could make any head-way the wind roared into the pressure ridge.

Russel drew the hood tight on his parka and huddled into the dogs, closing the small opening in the front of his hood by burying his face in dog fur.

The dogs whined for a few moments, then squirmed into better positions, with their noses under their tails, and settled in to ride the storm out the same way dogs and wolves have ridden storms out forever—by sleeping and waiting.

Russel felt a couple of small wind-leaks around the edge of his parka and he stopped them by pulling the drawstrings tighter at the parka's bottom hem. When he had all air movement stopped he could feel the temperature coming up in his clothing and he listened to the wind as it tore at his shelter.

In what seemed like moments but might have been an hour, the wind had piled a drift over his hole and he used a free arm to pack the snow away and clear the space around his body. The dogs remained still and quiet, their heat tight around Russel.

After a time he dozed, and when he awakened it seemed that the wind had diminished to some degree. He used a mittened hand to clear away a hole and he saw that it was getting darker—the short day almost gone again—and that indeed the wind was dying.

He stood, broke through the drift and shrugged the snow off. It was still cloudy but everything seemed to be lifting. The dogs were curled in small balls covered with snow, each of them completely covered except for a small blowhole where a breath had kept the snow melted. Each hole had a tiny bit of steam puffing up as the dogs exhaled and Russel was reluctant to make them stir. They looked so comfortable in their small houses.

Still he had to get home.

"Ha! Hay! Everybody up!" He grabbed the gangline and shook it. The leader stood up and shook his fur clean of snow and that brought the rest of them up. Slowly they stretched and three of them evacuated, showing they understood work. A good dog will always leave waste before going to work, to not carry extra on the run.

In a minute he had them lined out, aimed for home—or where he thought the village was—and when he called them to run they went about thirty yards and stopped. It wasn't abrupt. They were running and they slowed to a trot and then a walk and finally they just stopped.

"What is it?" Russel snorted. "Are we still asleep in our houses? Hai! Get it up and go."

Again they started and went forty or so yards and stopped.

Russel swore. "Get up! Run now or I will find a whip."

And after a time, hesitating still, they finally

got moving. Slowly. At a trot first, then a fast walk, then back up to a trot, they headed across the ice fields.

Russel nodded in satisfaction. He had not run dogs enough to know for certain what it meant when they didn't want to run, but he supposed that it was because they had anticipated staying down for a longer time.

But the man had to run the dogs. That's what Oogruk had said to him. "You must be part of the dogs, but you must run them. If you do not tell them what to do and where to go they will go where they want. And where a dog wants to go is not always the same as where the man wants to go."

The wind had stopped almost as suddenly as it came, in the way of arctic storms, but before it died it seemed to have changed a bit. When it first came it was out of the west, straight in from the sea, but before it stopped Russel noted that it had moved around to the north, was coming down from the blue-black north, the cold places.

Twice more the dogs tried to come to the right, but he made them go back and run his way. At last they lined out and went to work and Russel looked for the lights of the village. He had come out a way, but as the wind died he knew they should show, especially the light up on the hill near the fuel tanks.

He saw nothing. The clouds were still thick and low so he couldn't see the stars. He had nothing to help him tell his true direction.

He ran for several hours, letting the dogs seek their own speed, and once he was sure he should have run into the village he called them down and set the snowhook.

He was going the wrong way.

What has happened, he thought, is that during the storm the ice has caked and turned. A whole, huge plate of ice with Russel and the dogs had rotated and changed all his directions. That's why the dogs had hesitated, held back. They knew the way home and had wanted to head back to the house.

He could have let them run and they would have taken him home. But now—now what would they do?

More now, he thought. More is coming now. It was getting cold, colder than he'd ever seen it. He could feel the cold working into his clothing, see the white steam of the dogs' breath coming back over their backs. His feet were starting to hurt. He was lost and the cold was working in and he did not know where to go.

There were just the dogs—the dogs and the sled and him. And the ice, and the snow and the northern night. Nobody would come to look for him because they expected him to be out late—or didn't expect anything at all. He had told nobody other than Oogruk that he was going out for seals and since he was staying at Oogruk's house nobody else could know that he was gone. And Oogruk would not expect him back because Russel was hunting the old way.

He was alone.

And a part of him grew afraid. He had seen bad weather many times. But he'd always had the chance to get out of it. On a snowmachine, unless it broke down, you could ride to safety. But he would have to face the cold now.

He debated what to do for three or four minutes. If he went down without a fire the cold would get bad later—maybe too bad. He had nothing to burn and there was no wood or fuel on the ice.

And what had Oogruk said about that? He fought to remember the trance but nothing came. He knew about problems growing in the cold, or during a storm, from other people. But Oogruk had said nothing about being lost on the ice.

Lost on the ice.

People died when they were lost on the ice. He

had heard stories of people dying, of whole families lost. The ice moved out and away from land and the people had starved to death or drowned when the ice broke up beneath them, stories that came down in the long nights, sad stories.

And now Russel. Now Russel lost on the ice with a dog team and sled.

In the sled bag he had a small piece of meat left over from when he and Oogruk had cooked the deer. He could eat. That would help him stay warm. And then what?

He could wait until the clouds cleared off and he could see stars and they would guide him home. But it might be many days. Sometimes the clouds stayed for weeks.

"So." He talked aloud to the dogs, saw a couple of tails wag in the darkness with his voice. "So there is some trouble. What should we do?"

The leader looked around at him, although it was too dark for Russel to see his face. Still, there was something there, a desire to understand or to help. Russel smiled, a quick sign back in the fur of his hood.

The dogs.

They were the answer. He could not trust himself, couldn't see anything to help him, but he could trust the dogs. Or he thought he could. He would let them run and decide where to go.

"Hai! Enough rest. It is time to take me home. Take me back to the village."

He squeaked with his lips and they got up and started off. At first they traveled in the direction Russel had forced them to go. But as they settled into their trot the leader moved them gently to the right, more and more to the right until he had them going where he had first started them off before Russel had corrected him.

Russel nodded, let them run. They had a purpose in their backs, a pulling sense that he could believe in. He was learning about dogs, just in the few runs he'd taken. He was learning.

And one thing he had to know was that in some ways they were smarter than men. Oorgruk had said that to him.

"Men and dogs are not alike, although some men try to make them so. White men." Oogruk had laughed. "Because they try to make people out of dogs and in this way they make the dogs dumb. But to say that a dog is not smart because it is not as smart as a man is to say that snow is not smart. Dogs are not men. And as dogs, if they are allowed to be dogs, they are often smarter than men."

The problem, Russel knew, was learning when to recognize that dogs were smart. The dogs knew how to run in the dark and see with their heads, with their feet, with their hair and noses. They saw with everything.

At last Russel *knew* that they were heading back for the village in the cold and dark, knew it because he felt it inside.

But they were not home yet.

Running in the dark, even in the tight dark of the north when there is no moon, it is possible to see out ahead a great distance. The snow-ice is white-blue in the dark and if there is no wind to blow the snow around, everything shows up against the white.

Now, suddenly, there was a dark line ahead of the lead dog. A dark line followed by a black space on the snow, an opening of the ice. A lead of open water, so wide Russel could not see across.

Open water. Steam rising into the cold. The ice was moving and he was moving with it.

The team stopped. The lead dog whined and moved back and forth across the edge of the ice. The dogs hated open water, hated to get wet, but they knew that the way home was across the lead.

For a few moments the leader continued to whine and pull back and forth. "Haw! We go left along the ice and see."

The leader slammed to the left gratefully, happy to be relieved of the responsibility.

But the open lead was long. They ran mile after mile along the broken edge of the ice, in and out of the steam wraiths that came from the sea water. New ice was forming rapidly in the deep cold but it was not safe and would not be safe for several days, if then. Besides, it kept breaking away with the shifting of the cake that Russel was running on.

Yet the fear was gone. The fear had come from the unknown, from not acting, and now that he had made a decision to act the fear had gone. He might not make it, he might die on the ice, but he would not die with fear. He would die working to not die.

That was something he could tell Oogruk when he got back. If he got back. The thing with dying was to try to not die and make death take you with surprise.

And with the end of the fear came a feeling of strength. The cold was less strong along the lead because the warmth from the sea water came up as steam. The steam froze on everything, on the gangline and the sled and the dogs. Soon everything glistened with ice, even the dogs looked like jewels running ahead of him in the dark with the ice frozen on their backs.

It was a beauty he could not measure. As so much of running the dogs proved to be—so much of it had a beauty he saw and took into himself but could not explain.

And while he was looking at the beauty he saw that the lead had narrowed. There was still open water, but there were large chunks floating in it and the idea came to him of bridging the open water with one of the chunks.

He stopped the team.

The leader whined. It is perhaps possible that Oogruk has done this, Russel thought, and the dog is scared because he's done it before.

Or it was possible that the dog was reading Russel's mind and knew what they were going to do. Or it might be that the dog had figured out what had to be done on his own.

Whatever the reason, the dog knew and he didn't like it. Russel set the hook and took the harpoon with the line on it out of the sled. He walked to the edge of the lead, holding back to make sure he wouldn't break off the edge and fall in. Death would come instantly with the water. With the weight of the parka and pants wet, he would go down like a stone.

There were several chunks floating in the lead, which had now narrowed to thirty or so feet. Most of them were smaller than he could use, but one was about twenty feet long and four feet wide. It lay sideways, halfway across the opening.

He lay the harpoon line on the ice, in a small loop, and held one end with his left hand. With his right he hefted the harpoon and with an easy toss threw it across the large chunk of ice.

Then he tried to ease it back so that the butt end of the harpoon would hang up on an edge. It was harder than it looked and took him ten or twelve tries before the harpoon shaft caught in a small hole. When it drew tight the point jammed and he took up the strain until he had the weight of the chunk moving. Slowly he pulled the ice through the dark water, slowly and gently heaving on the great weight.

He gradually brought the chunk across the lead until the end butted against the edge he stood on, then, using the harpoon as a prod he jammed and pushed until the ice lay the long way across the lead.

When it was in position he went back to the sled and pulled out the hook. "Up! Up and across the ice."

The leader knew what he wanted, but he held back, whining louder now. The ice didn't look that steady, didn't look safe. He didn't move to the side, but he wouldn't go, either.

Twice more Russel urged him from the sled but

the dog wouldn't go and Russel threw the sled over on its side and walked to the front. The leader shook and crouched down but didn't move away. Russel took his mittens off and hung them by their cords behind his back. Then he grabbed a handful of hair on the dog's neck and another at the root of his tail and heaved the dog out onto the chunk.

The leader fought for balance, found it on the teetering ice, then drove with all his might for the other side of the lead, clawing and scrabbling.

So powerful was his tearing struggle that he pulled the next two dogs after him, and those three then pulled the rest of the team and the sled in a great leap onto the floating ice bridge.

Russel grabbed the handle as it went by and barely got his feet on the runners. A kick left, another to the right and the sled flew across the gap of water at the far end, splashed once as Russel threw his feet up to stay out of the water—and he was across.

Across onto the land ice. Off the floating pack ice. Safe.

Safe with the dogs. Safe and heading for the village. Safe and moving to where he could now see the light of the fuel tank on the hill. Safe out of the steam of the water and back on the solid ice.

5

Shamans had great power in the old times before the church came. They could make stones talk, and the snow, and I knew one once that had two heads that talked to each other. They fought all the time, those two heads, and finally it was said that one of the heads told the body to kill the other. This it did and of course that made the whole body die. Shamans had great power but they weren't always smart.

—an old woman's memory.

RUSSEL HAD moved away from life in the village but he was not rebelling. He was working toward something in his mind, not away from something he didn't like. He had moved in with Oogruk, but his father knew it and approved.

There was school, of course. He was not going to school but he was learning and everybody knew that; it would have been hard to stop him trying to learn what he wanted and needed to know and so nobody tried. It would not have been polite to try it and many considered Russel old enough to know what he was doing.

Life in the village went on as it had before. Men took snowmachines out on the ice to find seals, when they could get through the leads. Other hunters took other snowmachines back into the hills and found caribou, sometimes killing six or seven to bring back for other people who could not hunt.

In the long darkness house life took on a meaning that couldn't exist in the summer. Families sometimes moved in with each other for a time, played games, fought the boredom that could come with the semi-arctic night. The village had a game room with television and it was usually crowded with both adults and children, watching the outside world.

All but Russel.

And Oogruk.

Russel hunted caribou twice more but didn't get any meat either time. He saw them at a distance, but couldn't get the sled close enough to make a stalk and a kill. On the second attempt he set the hook, left the dogs, and with the bow worked up some small creek beds but the deer saw him before he could get close enough for a shot. He took rabbits and ptarmigan home each time, using a small net Oogruk had fashioned and showed him how to use. With the net, laying it on the ground and using a long line, he lured the birds with a handful of berries. When they were on the net he flicked it closed with a jerk of his wrist and caught five and six birds at a time.

So he made meat. Light meat. That's what Oogruk called it. And it was good meat, as far as it went. The small birds tasted sweet and were tender and soft, which suited Oogruk's poor teeth.

But the dogs needed heavy meat, heavy red meat and fat or they could not work, could not run long and hard.

And heavy meat meant deer. Caribou.

Or seal.

So it came on a cold clear morning that Russel decided to go out for seal again. It was still dark when he awakened and sat up on the floor but before he could get his pants on Oogruk was sitting up and had lighted the lamp.

"It is time for me to go out for seals again. For food for the dogs. I will go out on the ice."

Oogruk nodded. "Yes. Yes. I know that. But this time I will go with you."

Russel stopped, his bearskin pants halfway up. He looked at the old man. "To hunt seals?"

"That. And other things. There are certain things that must be done at this time and it is for an old man to do them when the time is right."

Russel waited but Oogruk said nothing further. Instead he stood, slightly stiff, and feeling with his hands found clothes on the side wall. He dressed in pants and mukluks and another squirrelskin underparka. Then he took down an older outer-parka, of deerskin, one with holes and worn places, and shrugged it on over his head.

"I have the good parka," Russel said. "Let me give it to you."

Oogruk shook his head. "Not this time. You keep it. You will need it and I won't. Go now and harness the dogs."

Russel finished dressing and went out for the team. They knew him now, knew him well, and greeted him with tails and barks when they saw him take the harness off the pegs. He laid the gangline out onto the snow and harnessed the team quickly, wondering why the old man wanted to go.

When the dogs were harnessed he took the weapons—two harpoons and one killing lance with a plain sharpened point—and tied them into the sled. When he turned back to the house Oogruk had come out of the door and was looking across the ice.

His milk-white eyes stared across the ice. But he was seeing nothing. Or, Russel thought, maybe he was seeing everything.

"I smell the sea out there," Oogruk said. "It is not too far today. The ice lets the smell come across."

"The dogs are harnessed."

"I know."

"Would you drive them?"

"No. I will ride. Put me in the sled and you drive."

Russel took his hand and put him in the sled, settling him back against the crosspieces at the back. When Oogruk was settled Russel pulled the hook and called the dogs up.

They tore away from the buildings and out across the ice. When he was away on the ice and the fire was burned out of them a bit he dragged the brake down and slowed them and looked back at the village.

Small gray buildings and caches on the dirty snow of the beach, with people here and there. Someone he did not recognize waved at him and he waved back. Dirty smoke came from chimneys and slid off with the wind and he watched as they moved away, picked up speed on the clean ice-snow, until he rounded the point heading north and the buildings were gone.

He waited for some kind of sadness to come but it did not, did not, and he turned back to the sled and the dogs lined out in front and he moved them over to the right a little, using a soft "Gee," to let them know it was a gentle turn. The sea was a blue line on the horizon when they crossed the high points and could see ahead.

Oogruk said nothing, but when they got within a couple of miles of the sea and the spray smell was heavy in the cold air he held up his mittened hand to signal a halt.

"There will be seals. Watch for seals." His voice was excited, hushed but alive. "They will be on the edge of the ice. Watch for them."

Russel looked out on the edge of the ice but saw no seals. The light was half gone now and he knew that he would have to leave the sled to hunt.

"I will leave you with the dogs and go out on foot."

But now Oogruk shook his head. "No. No. It is time to talk one more time and I must leave you. But I wanted to come out here for it because I missed the smell of the sea. I wanted to smell the sea one more time."

Russel looked down in the sled at the old man. "You're leaving me?"

"Yes. But first I must tell you what to do . . ."

"Where are you going?"

"It is time to leave," Oogruk said simply. "It is my time. But there is a thing you must do now to become a man. You must not go home."

"Not go home? I do not understand."

"You must leave with the dogs. Run long and find yourself. When you leave me you must head north and take meat and see the country. When you do that you will become a man. Run as long as you can. That's what used to be. Once I ran for a year to find good birds' eggs. Run with the dogs and become what the dogs will help you become. Do you understand?"

Russel remembered now when Oogruk had said he would take a long journey. He spoke quietly. "I think so. But you, what are you to do?"

"You will leave me here on the ice, out here by the edge of the sea."

"With respect, Grandfather, I can't do that. There is a doctor. Things can be done if something is bothering you."

Oogruk shook his head. "An old man knows when death is coming and he should be left to his own on it. You will leave me here on the ice."

"But . . ."

"You will leave me here on the ice."

Russel said nothing. He didn't help Oogruk,

but the old man got out of the sled himself. When he was standing on the ice he motioned Russel away. "Go now."

Russel couldn't. He held back, held the sled. "I will stay with you."

"You will go." The milk-eyes looked through him to the sea, to the snow, to the line of blue that was the sky. "You will go now."

And there was such strength in his voice that Russel knew he must go. He took the handlebar in one hand and pulled the hook, and the dogs surged away and Russel let them run without looking back. He went mile after mile, and finally he could stand it no more and he called the team around and headed back, his eyes scanning the ice in sweeps as they ran.

When they were still half a mile from where Oogruk had gotten off, Russel could see his small figure sitting on the ice and he smiled.

He would talk the old man into riding back to the village, that's all there was to it. The old man would come back and tell him more about living the old way, would sit at night and tell the stories that made the winter nights short.

But when he drew close he saw that Oogruk was sitting still. Very still. His hands were folded in his lap and his legs were stretched out in front of him and the eyes were open and not blinking with life.

Russel stopped the team before the dogs were close to Oogruk and walked ahead on foot.

Oogruk did not turn his head but stared out to sea, out past the edge of ice where his spirit had flown, out and out. His face was already freezing and there was some blown snow in the corner of his eyes that didn't melt. Russel brushed the snow away with his mitten, a small gesture he made unknowingly, and a place in him wanted to smile and another place wanted to cry. "You left too soon, Grandfather. I was coming back for you."

He stood for a time looking down at the dead old man. Then he thought of something and he went back to the sled and took the small harpoon with the ivory toggle point from the weapons lashing. He put the harpoon across Oogruk's lap so that it balanced on his knees.

"You will want to hunt seals. Use it well and make much sweet meat."

Then he went to the sled. The dogs were nervous. They smelled the death and didn't like it. The leader whined and fidgeted and was glad when Russel called them around and headed north.

Before he let them run he turned back to Oogruk one more time. "I will remember you," he said, then let the dogs go.

He would run north for a time, then cut across the ice and head northeast into the land. He had weapons and dogs and a good sled. The rest would come from the land.

Everything would come from the land.

PART TWO

THE
DREAMRUN

6

The Run

Out.

Into the sweeps, into the great places where the land runs to the sky and into the sky until there is no land and there is no sky.

Out.

Into the distance where all lines end and all lines begin. Into the white line of the ice-blink where the mother of wind lives to send down the white death of the northern storms.

Out.

Into the mother of wind and the father of blue ice.

Russel went out where there is nothing, into the wide center of everything there is.

Into the north.

His village lay on the northern edge of the tree line. Here and there in small valleys nearby there were scrub spruce, ugly dwarfed things torn and ripped by the fierce wind. But as the run went north even these trees vanished to be replaced by small brush and gnarled grass. Snow was scarce, blown, and the landscape looked like something from another planet.

Still there is beauty, Russel thought.

It was hard to believe the beauty of that torn and forlorn place. The small mountains—large hills, really—were sculpted by the wind in shapes of rounded softness, and the light . . .

The light was a soft blue-purple during the day, a gentle color that goes into the eyes and becomes part of the mind and goes still deeper and deeper to enter the soul. Soul color is the daylight.

At night, Russel knew, often the wind would die and go back to its mother and the cold would come down from the father of ice and the northern lights would come to dance.

They went from red to green and back again, moving across the sky in great pulses of joy, rippling the heavens, pushing the stars back, and were so grand to see that many people believed that they were the souls of dead-born children dancing in heaven and playing with balls of grass and leather.

Even in the wind there was beauty to Russel. The wind came from the north in a steady push that made the dogs work evenly, and the wind made the snow move, change into shapes that blended into the light of day and the soft glow from the sky at night.

Out.

When he'd gone far enough north along the coast to miss the village, Russel headed back into shore and moved up onto the land in a small gully, headed mostly north but slightly east.

He moved into the dark. He ran the dogs out and down. Ran them steadily for a full day, eighteen hours, letting them find the way. He stood on the sled's runners and moved to get away from what he knew, ran to get away from death sitting on the ice in Oogruk's form.

When the first dog started to weave with exhaustion, still pulling, but slipping back and forth as it pulled, he sensed their tiredness in the black night and stopped the team. He had a piece of meat in the sled, deer meat from a leg and he cut it in six pieces. When he'd pulled them under an overhanging ledge out of the wind and tipped the sled on its side, he fed them. But they were too tired to eat and slept with the meat between their legs.

He didn't know that they could become that tired and the knowledge frightened him. He was north, in the open, and the dogs wouldn't eat and they were over a hundred and fifty miles to anything. Without the dogs he would die.

Without the dogs he was nothing.

He'd never felt so alone and for a time fear roared in him. The darkness became an enemy, the cold a killer, the night a ghost from the underworld that would take him down where demons would tear strips off him.

He tried a bite of the meat but he wasn't hungry. Not from tiredness. At least he didn't think so.

But he knew he wasn't thinking too well, and so he lay down between the two wheel-dogs and pulled them close on either side and took a kind of sleep.

Brain-rest more than sleep. He closed his eyes and something inside him rested. The darkness came harder and the northern lights danced and he rested. He was not sure how long it might have been, but it was still dark when one of the dogs got up and moved in a circle to find a better resting position.

The dog awakened the remainder of the team and they all ate their meat with quiet growls of satisfaction that came from their stomachs up through their throats. Small rumbles that could be felt more than heard.

When they'd eaten they lay down again, not even pausing to relieve themselves. And Russel let them stay down for all of that long night. He dozed now with his eyes open, still between the two wheel-dogs, until the light came briefly.

Then he stood and stretched, feeling the stiffness. The dogs didn't get up and he had to go up the line and lift them. They shook hard to loosen their muscles and drop the tightness of sleeping long.

"Up now! Up and out."

Out.

They started north again, into a land that Russel did not know. At first the dogs ran poorly, raggedly, hating it. But inside half a mile they had settled into their stride and were a working team once more.

But they had lost weight.

In the long run they had lost much weight and it was necessary for Russel to make meat. He didn't know how long they could go without meat but he didn't think it could be long.

He had to hunt.

If he did not get meat the dogs would go down—and he was nothing without the dogs. He had to get food for them.

The light ended the dark-fears but did not bring much warmth. Only the top edge of the sun slipped into view above the horizon, so there was no heat from it.

To get his body warm again after the long night of being still he held onto the sled and ran between the runners. He would run until his breath grew short, then jump on and catch his wind, then run again. It took a few miles of that to get him warm and as soon as he was, the great hole of hunger opened in his stomach and he nearly fell off the sled.

The hunger lasted until he remembered the small piece of meat he hadn't eaten the night before. He found it in the inside pouch of his parka and ate it. His body heat had thawed the meat and made it soft enough to chew. It was bad meat, tough meat, but it tasted so good that it made his jaws ache.

And with the meat came energy. It rippled through him, up from his stomach like something alive, something hot.

The meat brought strength into his legs and arms and made his eyes sharp. He scanned the hills ahead, the low round hills with grassy sides and small gullies between. That would be where he'd find game. The birds would be on the hillside where there was no snow to eat, but close to the snow so they could fly to the white for protection. The rabbits would be high so they could see when the wolves came. There would be mice in the grass if nothing else. All food.

He headed for the hills and reached into the sled for the bow. When he had it out he stopped the dogs and strung it, marveling again at its beauty, the laminated strips of horn and bone and wood shining in the light.

He took the quiver up and strapped it over his shoulder, letting the dogs run again as he worked. He would hunt with the team, rather than stalk, and hope to get close enough to something for a shot.

And now there was luck.

In many of the hills there were smaller animals. Rabbits and ptarmigan, some small fox—which had a sweet-rich meat and were easy to kill—and the ever-present mice, or lemmings. But sometimes herds of caribou numbering several hundred head moved across the land, taking the grass where they could find it.

Such a herd lay in the gully in front of Russel and the dogs. The only way out for the caribou was to run over the team, or around it. The gully had steep sides with large drifts and the deer had foolishly cornered themselves. A pack of wolves could get into them and take many of them down before they could escape. Or a man could take them. But the deer would think only of running, not where they could run, just that they could run, in blind lines.

The dogs smelled them before Russel saw them. They had seen him take the bow out and they knew he was ready to kill and when they smelled the deer they turned off and headed for the gully where the herd grazed.

There were about a hundred and fifty deer within the confines of the drifts and when the animals at the outside edge saw the dogs coming they wheeled and tried to beat Russel to the opening.

But the dogs were strong and thin and fast and they caught the deer easily. When they ran toward him into the narrowest part, Russel jumped off the sled and got ready. The dogs kept going, crazy now for the smell of deer and the wild running of the herd as it came at them.

The caribou parted around the sled and the dogs wheeled to catch them, missing most, hitting a few with the ancient hamstring tear that ripped and crippled the deer's back leg, and four of these, staggering with bloodied back legs, came by Russel.

Falling, running, they tried to keep up to the other deer but they were doomed now, as doomed as if they had been hit by wolves, and the dogs were working to catch them and pull them down.

Russel took them with arrows, putting a shaft in each one, just in back of the shoulders. He watched the arrows streak into the light and enter the deer cleanly. First one, then the other, then the next two, and they ran-fell for another fifty yards before they went down, blood spraying from their mouths onto the grass and snow.

"My arrows are true," he said aloud. And then, in a poem-song:

> They brought the deer down,
> They helped the dogs to bring us meat.
> My arrows are true.

The dogs were on the deer now, stopping with the first one. Russel ran over to it to hasten the death by cutting its throat but he didn't have to. The eyes were already glazing with the end and he put grass in the deer's mouth, doing the same for the second, third and fourth ones, which were already dead.

Then he pulled the dogs off and tied them away from the four carcasses. There would be food for them, but all in good time.

He would set up camp and he would skin the deer out and cut the meat for easy carrying. Then he would eat and eat, he thought, and after he ate he would sleep, and then eat more. He'd never been so hungry and he could see that the dogs were the same. They were on the edge of eating each other, fresh with the blood smell and tough with the running.

He set up camp and skinned the deer. By now it was getting dark and he cut front shoulder meat for the dogs—a great piece for each—and took a fatty tenderloin from one deer for himself. He used some grass and dried sticks and a match from his sled bag to start a fire and he warmed the meat over the flames until it was pleasant—not hot, just heated. Then he took a chunk in his mouth and bit down and cut it off by his lips with the *ulu*, wolfed it down, then another, and another, until his stomach hurt with the meat.

He mourned not having a pot, but ate snow for water and this, with the blood in the warm meat, was enough moisture to help in digestion.

With his stomach full he put one deerskin on the ground, hair side down, and the other three on top with the raw sides touching. In between the layers he had a fur sleeping bag as warm as the warmest down and he crawled in as the short-lived sun bobbed back down for the long night.

Full-bellied dogs curled into balls in their harness, sleeping next to him. Russel pulled his head under the skins, took his parka and pants off and put them outside, inside out. The moisture from his perspiration would freeze during the sleep and he would scrape the ice off in the morning. With only his squirrel parka on he pulled back into the skins, took his mukluks off and left them inside the sleeping bag to warm up and dry out.

It was a home.

The sled, the dogs, the food, and more food to eat when he awakened.

It was a home.

It was as much of a home as his people had had for thousands of years and he was content. He closed his eyes and heard the wind gently sighing outside past the hides that kept him warm and snug.

It was a home and he let his mind circle and go down, the same way a dog will circle before taking the right bed.

What a thing, he thought—what a thing it is to

have meat and be warm and have a full belly. What a thing of joy.

And he slept.

And while he slept he had a dream.

7

The Dream

THERE WERE swirls of fog like steam off the water in the ice leads; thick fog, heavy fog, that would start to clear and close again, then clear a little more until finally he could see, could see, could see . . .

A skin shelter, a tent, on the side of the ocean. Inside there was an oil lamp, much like the one Oogruk had, burning a smoky yellow that lighted the faces of the people in the tent.

Two children were there. Small and round and wonderfully fat. They were eating of some fat red meat that Russel could not understand, didn't know, but knew as being important. He wanted to know what kind of meat they were eating because it was so red and had coarse texture and rich yellow fat. All over the children's faces and in their hair the grease shone and they were happy with it.

On the other side of the lamp sat a woman, young, round and shining beautiful. She was fat and had eaten of the meat but was done now and worked at tending the lamp. There was much honor in tending the lamp and she took pride in it. The flame was even, if smoky, and in the stone lamp-bowl there was the same yellow fat that was so important for him to name.

One other person was in the skin tent and he couldn't see who it was; it was a man, but he kept back in the shadows and would not come forward.

They were saying nothing, but the children laughed until the laughter was like a kind of music in the background and the woman looked at the man and smiled often. It was the kind of smile all men look for in women, the kind that reaches inside, and Russel felt warm to see it.

But he could not see the man and he did not know the meat, and they were important to him.

The fog came again, and this time when it cleared

the man was standing near the doorway in a parka. The parka was deerskin and he held a long spear with some form of black stone point, chipped black stone that was deep and shining dark. He was going out hunting and Russel knew, sensed, that he was going to hunt whatever had made the coarse meat and yellow fat and Russel wanted to go with him.

The woman kept smiling and the children kept laughing but the woman was worried and said something in a language that Russel could not understand. It was words, and they were similar to what he knew, but enough different so they didn't quite make sense to him.

As the man turned to leave the hut the woman said something to him and he stopped and looked at her.

Her eyes glowed at him and there was much fear in them, so much that Russel was afraid, and he knew that there was some fear in the man, too, but hidden.

Russel would not have known that except that he felt close to the man. More than close somehow.

The man left the tent and went out to harness dogs and they were already in harness, waiting for him, and they were dogs but they were more than dogs, too.

Great gray sides twitching, they stood like

shadows, with wide heads and heavy triangular jaws. Russel had never seen anything like the dogs in the dream. They were higher than the man's waist and had silent yellow eyes that watched everything the man did while he put his gear in the sled and got ready to leave, and the way they watched it was clear that they could either run or turn and eat him. It was up to the man.

He stood to the sled and Russel saw then that it was not of wood but all of bone and ivory, with large rib bones for the runners, and lashed with yellow rawhide. It shone yellow-white and rich in the night light, the color deep and alive, and when the man stepped on the runners the dogs lunged silently but with great speed and power and the fog closed again, swirled in thick and deep.

When it lifted the man was alone out on the sweeps. The stretch of land looked familiar, but there was something different in the dream and after a time Russel could see that it was the grass. Where the snow had been blown away the grass was taller and thinner, with pointed ends. It was bent over in wind, but not twisted like the tundra grass.

There was deeper darkness now and Russel watched as the man worked the dogs without making a sound. They were clearly hunting something, that much was sure, but what they were hunting Russel couldn't tell. He was amazed to see the man handle the dogs with no audible commands.

They ran to his mind, clean and simple. They went out into the sweeps and Russel watched as if from somewhere above, watched as they hunted in and out of the fog until finally, in a clearing, they found the fresh tracks of whatever they were hunting.

The gray dogs put their hair up and ran to the tracks nervously. They wanted to catch the smell but they didn't want to as well. They were still running to the man's mind and he made them follow the tracks but there was fear now.

Great fear.

The tracks were blurred, but huge, and Russel couldn't see what might have made them. He had never seen tracks like them, nor felt the fear that was in the man.

Then there was a shape before him and Russel fought to see it.

Some great thing it was, some great shape in the fog and then the mist was whirled away in a rush of wind and Russel saw two things clearly.

The animal was a woolly mammoth. Immense, it stood with shaggy hair, its giant domed head swaying, its great tusks curved toward the dogs. The small trunk whipped back and forth in anger and the red eyes tore through the fog like a demon's from the Below World.

The man was to kill the beast if he could, or the beast was to kill the man and the dogs, drive them into the snow and kill them.

That much Russel saw clearly and one more thing.

As the man grabbed the long killing-lance and jumped from the ivory and bone sled, the wind blew off his parka hood and Russel saw the man's face and knew it.

The man was him: Russel, with more hair, longer hair, and a small beard and mustache, but he was Russel and Russel knew fear, deep fear, because with the knowledge that he was the man in the dream he knew that he would have to fight the mammoth. He would have to fight it and kill it.

And the mammoth charged.

The head and tusks thrashed in angry arcs and the huge feet trampled the earth, tearing up clods of dirty snow, as the mighty animal bore down on the man and the dogs and sled.

There was no time for escape, no time for dodging. The man had to face the beast.

The dogs ran to the side, but turned back in as the mammoth rushed by them, heading for the man. But their action caused the animal to swing its head slightly to the side and that revealed the center of the chest.

Crouching and turned away, the man set the shaft of the long lance in the earth and snow in back of him, settled it in as hard as he could and rose to face the oncoming mammoth. With its head sideways to lash at the dogs it roared down on the man as with small arm movements he guided the point of the lance into the center of the chest and let the weight of the animal carry it down the shaft to death.

The lance entered like light, like a beam of light shot into the mammoth and when there should have been death the animal instead wheeled and heaved in a great circle, caught the dogs and threw two of them in the air.

All in silence.

And then the beast stopped. It stood with its head hanging, swaying back and forth, and accepted the death from the broken lance shaft in its chest and went down on its front knees and then its back and in an almost gentle roll slipped to its side and died.

And the man as he saw the animal falter began to sing. Again Russel did not know the words but they sounded familiar to him.

The man sang in exultation.

Sang the death of the great beast, and the mountain of meat lying before him.

Sang the luck of his hunt.

Sang of the fat that would be his for his family and the dogs that now tore at the belly of the mammoth.

Sang the wind that brought his dogs to the tracks and sang the gratitude for the great animal who died and left him much meat.

And Russel felt all those songs inside his soul, felt them even as the man in the dream sang and the fog came again to hide him and the dogs and the mammoth.

Russel knew it all because he knew them all. He was the man and he was the dream.

He was the fog.

8

The Run

THE LIGHT filtered into the skins and he awakened. Some of the dream was still with him and he had a great hunger for the coarse red meat and yellow fat but when he looked out from the skins he saw only the four deer carcasses. The team was chewing on one.

He stuck an arm out and scraped his parka and turned it right side out and put it on. The cold of the skin penetrated his squirrelskin undergarment and brought him totally, instantly wide awake.

Next he put his mukluks on—they were warm from being in the skins all night—and then he threw back the skins and stood.

The dogs had fought while he dreamed and the gangline was bitten in two or three places. He swore and pulled them back from the deer and to the sled and tied them in place, liberally slamming their noses with his mittened hand.

In a few moments they had settled and he went back to the deer. Their bodies had frozen but were small enough to fit roughly on the sled. Legs stuck out but he wanted to keep going and the legs didn't bother him. There were no trees to catch at them.

The skins were more of a problem. Though he had slept in them the raw sides had frozen solid. The hollow hairs had kept his body heat from penetrating the skins and they would not fold. He finally jumped on them in the middle to fold them over and jam-fit them next to the deer carcasses on the sled.

He pulled his hood on, tightened it against the coming wind and called the dogs up. In minutes he was out of sight of the camp area, heading still north. Out. Into the sweeps.

Today was different—as Russel knew all days are different in the north. It was so cold his spit bounced—white men would call it forty below zero—and the air caught in his throat as he warmed it.

The color was new as well. Yesterday had been blue. Today was almost a deep purple with stringers of clouds shooting across the dimly lighted sky, fingers aimed away from an advancing storm.

Russel knew weather as all Eskimos know weather. The storm would come in two days, maybe a little less, but it would not be too bad. Some wind and cold, nothing more. He could ride it out easily.

But there was a strange unease driving him and at first he thought it was the dream. It had been so real-seeming. He could still smell the inside of the dreamigloo-tent, the stink of the mammoth voiding itself in death, the heat of its blood down the shaft of the lance.

He had killed the beast and yet something was pushing him, making him drive the team. They were new now, a new team. It wasn't that the dogs had changed; and yet they were not the same dogs that he'd first seen at Oogruk's. They changed with him, or at least so it seemed, changed with his mind.

It was as if they had gone out of themselves and become more than dogs, more than animal.

They ran to his mind, out and out before him.

With bellies full of deer meat, rich guts and stomach linings, the dogs were strong and driving, had great power, and wanted to run.

He let them run and they seemed to want to head the same way he wanted to go and that, too, became part of his thinking.

Did they know him?

Did they know his mind and run to it the way the wolf-dogs had run to the man's mind in the dream?

And if that were so, which he believed since he seemed to see his thoughts going out ahead, with the lead dog—if that were so, did the dogs know where they were going? Did they know when he didn't know?

And more, did they know *why* they were heading north?

"Why do we run?" he asked aloud and the sudden words broke the silence and startled the dogs. They kept running but broke stride for a few steps before regaining rhythm.

They did not answer.

Twice he looked back but saw nothing and after that he didn't look to the rear again. Out ahead was everything, out ahead was where they were going and he let the dogs decide because that was the same as his deciding.

The snow was right for speed, didn't have the cold-weather scrubbing sound it sometimes did which pulled at the runners, and they ran the daylight out without losing pace.

For five, maybe six, hours he let them run and as the gray dusk was gathering before dark he saw off to the right a small valley between two hills where there was some brush which might make a fire.

He said nothing to the team but they knew and they curved off to the right to head for the valley. There was still light as they came to it. He stopped them near some dried brush, dead in the wind and snow, but the dogs kept pulling forward and he let them go again. Further up there was an overhanging ledge of stone, a shelf, with a place under it to make a shelter. The dogs stopped when they reached the overhang.

He used one skin to shield the opening and scraped enough snow to secure it to the ledge. Then he cut a set of front shoulders up and threw the pieces to the dogs and pulled a second carcass into the lean-to. With the other skins he fashioned a bed and went out and collected bits of brushwood until he had enough to last the night and a little extra.

It was a perfect camp.

He brought the wood into the shelter and pulled the flap down. Using a bit of moss he started a small fire and in moments it was warm inside the shelter. He took his parka off and turned it inside out and put it back outside to freeze.

He heard the dogs growl, but they settled the problem immediately and he turned to warming meat to eat. Using the point of his knife he pried a tenderloin off the middle back of the carcass and held it over the small flame. The smoke was bad at first but he opened a hole at the top of the lean-to and the smoke was quickly sucked out by the wind.

The meat thawed in the flame and was soon warm enough to eat and he put the piece in his mouth and cut it off by his lips.

He was thirsty and he ate more snow with the meat, alternately chewing meat and eating snow until his stomach started to bulge.

He could eat no more yet he was hungry still. He thought of the red coarse meat of the dream, of the rich yellow fat and he closed his eyes.

But there was not sleep at first. Instead he thought of the day's run, then thought of Oogruk asking if they ran for him. It was a pleasant thought and Russel lay back on the hide to rest—but there was a lump beneath his shoulder. He was about to ignore it, to leave it there, but it was such a perfect camp that he wanted the bed to be perfect as well and he folded the skin back to see what the lump was. There was a stone there, a curved piece of stone, and when he pulled at it, it wiggled a bit.

He took his knife and dug around the edge, pulled at it, loosened it more, then dug again. Finally it came free and when it was in his hand he saw that it was more than a stone. It was a stone that had been worked by hand.

It was round, a disc about ten inches in diameter, and smoothly polished. On one side it was completely flat, but on the other it had been hollowed out to form a six inch dish, one edge of which had a small groove in it.

It was an old stone lamp. Older, much older than Oogruk's. Older than the lamps in the museums he had seen that were dug by the college people from the old village up north. Somebody had camped here many years before and either left the lamp or had come upon a disaster which ended what they had been. Only the lamp was left, and Russel held it and wondered at the shiny smoothness of it, the polished beauty.

"See what a man has been given," he said. "By the dogs who brought me. By the night. See what a man has been given." He had dropped into the third person usage without thinking, though it was no longer used very much. He had heard the old people talk that way sometimes out of politeness.

He used the back of his knife to scrape the last of the dirt off the lamp and set it aside. He needed some fat to light it and he went outside once more to the caribou carcass to get stomach fat.

"The best fat to eat is the best fat to burn," Oogruk had said. "Save the best for the flame and you will never be cold. It is a good lesson for a man. Save the best for the flame."

Russel took the stomach fat, pried it off with his knife—it was still frozen—and cut it in chips for the lamp bowl. When he had a small mound of chips he found some moss near the ledge and fashioned a wick. Then he took a burning stick from the fire and tried to light the lamp.

It was necessary to melt the fat into a puddle in the lamp so that as a liquid it could be wicked-up into the moss for burning.

After a good hour of moving the chips around and becoming frustrated he was ready to give up. But he tried once more and was rewarded when the chips of white fat suddenly became fluid and soaked into the moss. Smiling, he lit the wick and set the lamp on a small dirt ledge to the side of the shelter.

The fire died to embers but the lamp glow remained and the sweet yellow of the burning fat kept the night away, kept him warm. The fat was poor, he knew, compared to walrus fat or seal oil. And it burned with some smoke, though much less than the wood fire. But he did not need wood now, as long as he had deer for the fat. And there were many deer.

He could get everything from the deer.

He was sleepy now, again full and round with heat and food. But he didn't know how long the fat would last, or the wick, so he went outside and spent some time getting more fat from the same carcass. When he had a fair small pile of it, cut in chips, he found some more moss and twisted it into wick for later.

He added some chips to the liquid in the bowl and they melted and he saw that it was easy now to keep the level of the liquid up to the edge. Small crackles of rendered fat floated there and with quick fingers he dipped them out and ate them as they cooled.

He took a thin piece of wood and made a scrape-tool to keep the wick even. Then he lay back on the skins as the storm came up and he looked to all he had done and knew Oogruk would have liked it. Where there had been nothing he now had shelter and food and heat and comfort. Where there had been nothing he had become something.

The dogs were fed and down for rest, fed on meat and fat, fed on running and cold, fed and down.

He could sleep now. He would awaken in the night at intervals to add chips of fat to the lamp or to trim the wick, or perhaps to warm and eat a piece of meat or open a leg bone to get at the marrow, which tasted like the butter at the village store, or swallow a bit of snow when thirst took him.

He could sleep now.

And dream.

9

The Dream

HERE NOW was a village. The man drove his dogs out of the fog, the great gray dogs out of the gray fog, as if the dogs were not animals but fog that had come alive. Out they came onto a clearing on top of a bluff overlooking a coastal village, and the man set his bone snowhook.

There were many skin tents along the beach-ice, each tent by a meat rack filled with black blood-meat from walrus and seal. Steam from the heat was coming from the breathing holes on the tents, and though it was dim he saw children playing with puppies near the tents. It was a good camp. All the puppies were fat, and the dogs had good hair and were fat.

In the dream Russel could see over the man, could see how his mind was working and he knew that the man was holding back above the village out of sadness.

The camp was nothing he knew but the playing children and the sounds of women calling to each other through the tent walls made him think of the family he had left when he'd gone to hunt.

He was in a new land but the people were known to him as all people are known to all other people and their words made him think of his own family and he missed them, and for a moment Russel thought he might turn the team and head for home with the red meat and yellow fat.

But the dogs were excited and they jerked the snowhook free and tore down the hill with the ivory and bone sled flying behind like a feather in the wind. They wanted to meet the new dogs and perhaps fight and breed and eat and rest and they pulled the man down into the settlement on the beach.

Everybody came running out of the tents, half-dressed, yelling at the dogs to stop them from fighting, for the man's dogs were among the loose village dogs, snapping and barking, the sled behind them. After much whipping and yelling the dogs were separated.

There was great joy in the village. Visitors came very seldom and strangers almost never. The man had come from far away—they knew that from his dogs which were of a strange bloodline—and he was surely a mighty hunter because his sled was full of meat and his dogs were sleek and well fed even though they had come a long distance.

The new man would have stories to tell, wonderful stories of taking the large beast and traveling through strange lands. They would show the stranger their hospitality by feeding him much fat meat and feeding his dogs until they threw the meat up to eat it again.

Then they would take him into the main tent and they would talk and talk and perhaps later they would sing and dance to the drum and make up songs. Perhaps the stranger would sing his song.

It would be a night to last many days, with eating and eating until nothing more could be put down. A great time.

A new folding.

When it cleared Russel was inside a great tent. There were many people in the tent, sitting around the outside in a circle with the women back on a ledge.

There were a dozen or so lamps burning so that their light made the tent bright, hot-yellow with hazy smoke, and in the middle of the tent with his back to Russel stood the man who had come on the sled with the great gray dogs.

He wore only a breechclout held by a thin leather thong and Russel could see the knotted muscles in his back and down his legs, cords of power. His skin shone with sweat and grease from rubbing his hands on his body to clean them while he ate and his hair hung down in straight lines, heavy with grease.

He is not a man standing on the ground, Russel thought—he is growing up *from* the ground. His legs are the earth and they take strength from it, up through his ankles and into his muscles so that he grows with what he takes from it. More than strength, more than substance—all that the man would be is growing up from the earth through his legs and into his body.

Strong.

Strong beyond what he was merely, the man

had grown strong from the dogs and the wind and the winter and strong from the people around in a circle who watched now, watched and waited.

The man kept his back to Russel but Russel knew why and didn't care. He knew that he was the man, knew it and let that knowledge carry him into the man.

And now the man started to move.

His legs shuffled and his head swung from side to side and his hair moved with his body and he was not a man anymore.

He was the mammoth. It was more than a dance, more than a story, he *became* the mammoth, down to the smell, the foul smell that came from the beast.

The man moved and the mammoth moved and the people swept back to avoid being trampled, moved back in fear and some children who had no manners cried out in fear that the beast would see them.

But there was sadness here. For the mammoth knew that he must die, knew that he must furnish meat for the man. And so he knew he must run down the lance and give his death for food. There was sadness in his dance. In his movement.

The man sang and Russel could not understand the words but he knew their meaning: it was the song of the beast, the mammoth's song as he moved to his death at the hands of the puny man with the dogs. It was a noble song, a song to proclaim that he did not really have to die but chose to because it was his time and he would die with rightness, die correctly.

Sadness.

A rich sadness that took the man and made everybody watching feel deeply for the plight of the mammoth, cursed to death to make meat.

But now there was something new.

Now the mammoth grew, took strength and rage. Around the circle the man moved-danced, his voice growing through the song of the mammoth as it first saw the dogs and man.

And in the way of such things it had to attack. There was no sense to it because the mammoth could have kept going away. But the beast turned. In rage it attacked the dogs and turned its head to hit them and ran upon the lance.

Sometimes a man would be wrong and the lance would miss or hit the shoulder and slide off to the side and the man would die, would be trampled to death. Then it was not the time for the mammoth to die but time for the man to die and Russel knew this, knew all of this because of the movements of the man in the dream.

Now he changed again and now he was himself, the man, dancing and moving to kill the mammoth.

And now the beast charged.

And now he ran on the lance.

And now he died.

And it was all in the man and all in the people who watched and all in the small space in the council tent, all of it.

When the song was done the children screamed for joy and hunger at the meat he had brought and the men nodded and grunted approval at his mighty hunting and the women moved for him to attract his eye, because he was a hunter of such stature.

The man fell to the floor exhausted and they left him there, at the side, while somebody else rose to dance his song of a kayak and a walrus and near-death in the water.

And when he was done another got up, and then another, and so the songs soared on and on through day and night as the dream folded back into the fog.

10

The Run

WHEN THE STORM hit his shelter it awakened him and he listened for a time. But he was secure and had fat for the lamp and he went back to sleep—the best way to ride storms out in the arctic.

When he awakened the next time—perhaps twenty hours later—he was ravenous and thirsty, and outside it was still. He looked from the shelter and saw that the dogs were still sleeping, resting, and would remain so until he called them up. He was learning. If they worked hard they might sleep for three days, getting up just to relieve themselves and change position—not even that if the wind was bad and they had good snow caves made for shelter.

Russel took snow in and ate from it, mourning once more his lack of a pot for cooking and boiling and making water from the snow. He fashioned a ladle from a leg bone but got only sips for his work.

He added fat chips to the lamp, which was halfway empty, and they melted and he found that by pushing the wick further into the fluid fat the flame rose.

He used the expanded flame to heat a piece of loin from the deer and when it was warm ate it in large mouthfuls.

It didn't fill him and he ate some warm fat, then more meat and yet more fat until his stomach bulged and he was again full.

But this time sleep didn't come. He had slept the better part of two days now and no part of his body was tired enough to sleep more.

He looked out of the tent again and saw that daylight was coming.

He shrugged away the camp as he would shrug

away light snow. It was time to leave, time to head north again to see the father of ice. He brought his parka in, brushed off the frozen sweat and put it on. Then he pinched the flame out with his fingers and slide his mukluks on and stepped into the darkness. It took him just a few moments to take down the skins, softened now from the heat of the lamp, and fold them in the sled bottom, then the lamp in the sled bag, and finally the rest of the meat on top of the skins and, lastly, his weapons: the lance and harpoon shafts on top of the skins, then his bow and the quiver of arrows. None of the deer had broken arrows when they fell and he had cleaned the points of the bubbled blood that comes from a kill and put them back in the quiver.

Still the dogs weren't moving.

When everything was lashed down to the sled, Russel went up the line and jerked the team out of the snow.

Two of them growled and he slapped them with a mitten across their noses to get their attention.

When they were all up and standing he got on the sled and called them up.

They started slowly, two of them holding back until he yelled at them again. Then they went to work and headed away from the camp.

Light came gently, but the sky was clear and cold and clean and he let the dogs seek their own pace. Once they had shaken out their legs they began an easy lope that covered miles at a fierce clip.

They ran into light, then all through the day, easily pulling the sled on the fast snow, grabbing a mouthful when they got thirsty, and Russel watched the new country come.

There were few hills now. The land was very flat, and there were no trees of any kind. If he kept going this way for a long time—he was not sure how long it would take with dogs but it took all day with an airplane—he would come to mountains. He thought.

But before the mountains he believed the sea came back in again. In the school he had seen a map that showed the sea coming back into the land but he was not sure if that was straight north or north and west and he was not sure how long it would take to get to the sea by dog sled. He did not know how far dogs traveled in a day.

Yet it didn't matter.

Oogruk had said, "It isn't the destination that counts. It is the journey. That is what life is. A journey. Make it the right way and you will fill it correctly with days. Pay attention to the journey."

So Russel ran the team and now the land was so flat that it seemed to rise around him like a great lamp bowl sloping up to the sky.

Looking ahead, he could feel a small grit coming to his eyes, sensed the first stages of snow blindness—caused when the light comes from all directions, from the white snow and the flat blue sky. When it is very bad it's as if someone has poured sand in the eyes and it's impossible to open them to see. More often snow blindness just irritates.

Russel rubbed his eyes. He knew if he had wood he could make a pair of snow goggles, with small slits to cut out the light from the sides. But he didn't have wood, so he rubbed his eyes now and then and pulled his hood tighter.

When the short day was gone the dogs didn't seem to want to stop. He let them run. There was no place to camp anyway and his mind looked now to the run.

He had come north a long way but was not sure how long. In the dark they kept up the pace, increased it, and they could cover many more miles before he had to rest them again, running on fresh meat as they were.

He sensed in the night that he was passing a large herd of deer and the dogs started for them but he had meat and called them back to the north. They obeyed instantly and he felt good.

They were his now. They were his dogs and they would run to him. He made the meat for them and they would run to him—just as the dogs in the dream ran to the man. Just as they ran, his dogs would run.

Out into the night he ran, and through the other side of darkness.

It was coming into first light when he saw the snowmachine tracks.

They started as if by magic. Suddenly the snow bore the small ridges that come from a snowmachine.

They headed off to the north.

The dogs dropped into the line of the tracks easily, as they dropped into any trail, which surprised Russel. Given a chance they seemed to follow the path of least resistance as if they expected something.

Russel let them run and thought for a time. He knew quite an area, had once flown to a northern settlement, a village three hundred miles up the coast from his own.

But he could not think of a settlement that fit

with the tracks. There was nothing straight north. If the tracks were a hunting party from the village, it was way out of the normal hunting territory— and besides, Russel thought, anybody hunting now would be working the sea ice for seals.

He did not want to see anybody, especially somebody on a snowmachine. The idea of a snow-machine was out of place, opposite, wrong.

But.

It was possible that whoever it was might have an extra pot or can he could use. He sorely missed having a way to boil meat or make water from snow and his lips were starting to crack and bleed from the snow's sharpness. If he did not find a way to melt snow his lips would soon go to sores.

Oogruk had talked of using stone bowls to melt snow but Russel couldn't find the right kind of soft stone and so he hoped to find a pot or a can.

And there was the other thing. He was starting to notice the dogs, notice that they seemed to be an extension of his thoughts. Now they ran to the trail and perhaps that was because he wanted them to run to the trail.

Perhaps he wanted to see whoever it was, see where the tracks led. So he let them run the snow-machine trail and they lasted through that day and into the night and still he ran. The tracks led steadily to the north, the line moving out to the rim of the white saucer into dark and then out of sight into the blackness.

Always north.

He let the dogs run, stopping in the cold dawn to feed them some meat, taking a cold mouthful for himself, then eating some snow, wincing in pain from his cracked lips, and moving them on.

He saw no game that day, no other sign but the snowmachine tracks with the slight dusting of snow on the edges, filling in as the wind blew, and he debated stopping.

But the dogs wanted to run and he let them.

They ran the second night, and he did not sleep but his mind circled and slipped down as he rode the runners, tired but not tired. He quit thinking, quit being anything but part of the sled, part of the dogs. At one time he began to hallucinate and thought somebody was riding the sled in front of him, sitting in the basket. A blurred idea of someone.

But then the hallucination was gone and another one came; he saw lights on all the dogs' feet, small lights, and then they disappeared and he felt somehow that the opening of his parka hood was a mirror and everything he saw in front of him was somehow in back of him, and then, driving on into the night, the mirror vanished and he had the dream.

The dream again.

But darker.

II

The Dream

THE MAN WAS no longer in the settlement on the edge of the sea, fat with walrus and seal oil, among fat puppies and round dogs and round faces.

Now there was not a fog, but a slashing gray storm that took everything.

He was trying to drive his dogs in the storm and there was an air of madness to it. The wind tore at them, lifted their hair and drove the snow underneath it to freeze on their skin until the dogs were coated in ice. Icedogs. They shone through the snow as they tried to drive forward.

But the wind tore at them. The dogs were blown sideways so hard that they leaned to stand and when they hit patches of ice or frozen snow they went down, staggering.

Yet the man drove them.

He stood on the runners, screamed blindly at them, let the long whip go out to tear at their flanks. His will flew along the line to the dogs, pushing them fiercely into the roaring storm.

Russel could see no sense to it. The sled was full of the red meat, the man could stop and make a shelter and eat and feed the dogs and wait for the storm.

But there was terrible worry in the man, fear and worry that Russel could feel, up from the dream into his mind, into his soul, and when he let his mind go into the dream, into the man, he knew the reason.

He had stayed long at the village with the fat of seal and walrus. Perhaps too long. And now the journey home was taking too long, too long for the family that waited back in the skin tent for the red meat and fat.

The storm was stopping him. He could fight

and fight, whip the dogs until they ran red with blood, but the storm was stopping him.

It was too fierce. Now it blew the dogs sideways, and now it blew them backward and they felt the frustration of the man and it became anger and they fought among themselves, tearing and slashing.

The man used his whip handle like a club and beat them apart and settled them and admitted defeat, fell in the wind, fell next to the sled and huddled in his parka as the gray blasts of snow took him down and down . . .

The wind took the dream with snow as the fog had once taken it, closed on it. But now the dream wasn't finished . . .

From Russel's mind came the tent with the woman and the two children. But now they were not the same . . . Now the lamp flickers with the last of the oil and the faces are thin. Worse than thin, the children's faces have the deep lines and dark shades that come from starvation.

Both children lie quietly on the sleeping bench, end to end, their heads together. They are very weak, weak perhaps beyond coming back.

The mother sits by the lamp, fingering the strangulation cord. There are no skins left. They have eaten them all. They have eaten all the skin clothing and the soles from their mukluks and the leather lines cut to use for tying dogs.

They have cut the mittens into small squares to chew on the skin, spitting the hair out, and now those are gone.

Everything is gone.

And outside, the storm still tears and rips the earth, drives the snow sideways, guts the land.

She would eat the skin of the tent but that is the same as dying. With the tent gone the wind and cold would have them. They have no clothing left, will have no oil left when the lamp goes out.

Nothing.

The mother is weaker than the children but she takes a finger now and wipes it in the small bit of rancid oil in the lamp and wipes the finger across the lips of each child, leaving a thin film of grease on each lip.

One child licks the grease off.

The other does not.

And outside, the wind slashes and looks for their lives.

The hungry wind.

12

The Run

He came upon the snow-machine in the flat white light of the arctic dawn. It was sitting on its skis, just squatting in the middle of the great sweeps.

Nobody was near it. Russel stopped when the dogs were next to it and set his hook. On the back of the seat was a box and he opened it, hoping to find a coffee can or pot but there was nothing but an empty plastic gas jug.

He felt the engine with a bare hand. It was cold, still cold, dead cold.

It was a fairly new machine and while it was true that snowmachines broke down, the newer ones tended to last a bit longer. He opened the gas tank and found it bone dry.

A smile cut his lips and made them bleed.

"They are not of the land," he said to the dogs. "They need fuel that is not part of the land. They cannot run on fat and meat."

A small set of footprints led off ahead of the machine but there were also snowmachine tracks. It was as if another snowmachine had gone ahead, but left the person to walk. It made no sense.

Or. Perhaps the snowmachine had come out this way and the rider was headed back when the machine ran out of gas.

That made more sense to Russel, considering the tracks.

But there was nothing, no village, where the footprints were leading. Nothing that Russel knew about at any rate, and if whoever left the tracks was heading for help on foot he had almost no chance of getting anywhere. There were no settlements within walking distance of the snowmachine.

And the tracks were small enough to belong to a child. Or a girl.

He pulled the hook and the team started off silently. They had run steadily now for two days and needed rest. They could sleep running, a doze-sleep, but they needed real rest after the hard work of a long run.

But with the full light Russel could see the high wisps of clouds that meant a storm was coming.

He wanted to try to catch whoever was ahead before the storm hit. On foot he could not be carrying much of a shelter, nor could he be carrying much food. And if it was a child he would probably not survive a bad storm.

Russel let the dogs adopt a slower trot, but he kept them going steadily, watching the tracks ahead.

At first they didn't seem very fresh. The rising wind had blown them in so that some of them were filled completely. But as the hours passed they seemed to be getting cleaner, newer. Now and then the lead dog dropped his nose to smell them, looking for scent, and Russel could see his ears jerk forward whenever he got a bit.

And when the darkness came again the leader started to run with his nose down all the time, following the smell of the trail that must be fresh, Russel knew, to hold for the dogs.

But now there was wind and more wind. Not

as bad as the dreamwind, but getting worse all the time so that the dogs had to lean slightly left into it to keep their balance. And snow.

There was a driving sharp snow with the wind. Not heavy snow, but small and mean and it worked with the force of the wind to get inside clothing, in the eyes, even blow up into the nostrils.

And finally, when he could no longer see the trail, no longer see the front end of the team, could barely make out the two wheel-dogs directly in front of the sled, finally he came to that time when he should stop and hole up in the storm.

And he did not.

He drove them on. They wanted to stop, twice the leader did stop, but Russel used words as a whip and drove them.

The leader was all important now. The trail was gone, wiped away by the wind and snow in the dark, but the dog sensed with his nose and his feet where the tracks lay and he followed them. Russel almost did not believe the dog could do this—almost, but not quite. Had it happened earlier, when he first started to run the team, back at Oogruk's, he would not have believed. But now he understood more of the dogs, knew that they had understanding he did not have. Yet.

And he believed in the dogs.

The only advantage they had was that the storm was almost straight out of the north. They could fight dead against the wind and that was a bit easier than going side-on where the team would have been blown over.

But it was hard. And the storm, it seemed, worsened by the minute. At length Russel sensed that they were going up a slight incline, not a hill so much as a gradual upgrade, and at the top the dogs stopped dead in the wind.

He yelled at them, swore at them, finally began slamming the sled with his mittened hand and threatened to come up to the unseen dogs and beat them into submission.

But they would not move.

So they are done, he thought. He would have to make a shelter and ride the storm out. But first he would walk to the front of the team and bring the leader back around and use the dogs to form a part of a shelter.

He staggered against the wind to the front of the line and as he reached down for the collar on the lead dog he tripped and fell on something in the trail.

When he had recovered he saw that it was a booted foot, attached to a leg, and by moving up along the leg he found a person with a parka lying curled up, face away from the wind, extremely still.

He shook the figure with his hand but there was no response and he thought the person must be dead.

So much death, he thought. Oogruk and now this person. So much death given in this hard place.

But as he turned away he saw the arm move, or thought he saw some movement, and when he looked back he was sure of it—the bulky form had some life. Somewhere inside the round shape huddled on the trail there was a living person.

There was little time now. Whoever it was, the life was almost gone. There had to be a place to live now, a warm place, and Russel worked as fast as he could without sweating. Sweat, of all things, could kill. Steadily, evenly, he brought the dogs around and placed them down with his hands in a living screen across the face of the wind. They would soon be covered with snow and warm in their small igloos.

Then he took the skins from the sled and using the sled basket as one wall made a tent lean-to of two skins, folding one with the hair in to make a floor. The wind took the tent down twice, pulling the skins out and away so that he had to fight hard to keep them. But at last, using some bits of cord from the sled bag, he tied the skins down at the corners to the sled and packed snow around them and they held. The wind would blow more snow in and pack them still further.

Then he put the lamp and a partial carcass into the lean-to and went back for the figure in the snow. It took much heaving, pulling on the feet, to get the unconscious person into the lean-to and reclose the flap so the wind wouldn't tear it open. But he succeeded at last and fumbled with matches to get the lamp going. It started slowly, casting only a tiny flicker of light, until the fat around the wick began to melt and when it was going at last and he could feel some heat coming from it he turned to his companion.

When he pushed the hood back he was stunned to see that it was a girl. Woman, he thought— girl-woman. She had a round face with the white spots that come from freezing, and pitch-black thick hair pulled back in a bun and held with a leather thong.

He rubbed her cheeks but there was no response and yet he could see that she was breathing. Small spurts of steam came up in the cold yellow air in the lean-to. There was life inside the frozen shell.

He tore off her outerparka. Really it was a light

anorak made of canvas, and underneath she had on a vest. When the parka was off he realized that she was not only a young woman but that she was pregnant.

This realization stopped him and he settled back on his haunches to think of it. There were so many strange things here. She was where she couldn't possibly be, riding a snowmachine that had run out of gas, with no supplies, coming from nowhere and going nowhere.

She couldn't be.

And yet she was.

And she was pregnant and nearly dead.

He chipped some pieces of fat off the deer carcass and added them to the lamp. He did it several times while he thought on what to do. Soon the lamp was full of fat and he remembered the dream, remembered the woman trying to save the children from starvation.

He took his finger and dipped it in the fat of the lamp and wiped it across the blue lips. There was no indication from the woman-girl at all. He did it again, and again, until some of the fat had worked into her mouth and then he saw the jaw move. Not a swallowing, not a chewing, but a ripple in the jaw muscle.

She was coming back.

Soon the pain would hit her. When somebody has gotten close to death by freezing and he comes back, Russel knew, there is terrible pain. Sometimes it was possible to relieve the pain by rubbing snow on the frozen parts but when it was the whole body nothing helped.

The pain had to be. It was considered by some—by Oogruk—to be the same pain as birth. To have been close to death and come back could not be done without the pain of birth.

Russel sat back again, then cut some meat and held it over the flame. After the pain would come hunger. She would want to eat. As he wanted to eat.

The meat softened with the flame and when it had taken on some warmth he ate part of it. Doing so made him think of the dogs and he considered cutting them food but decided to let them sleep for a time first. They had run long and were probably too tired to eat.

Instead he ate some more meat and watched the woman-girl he had rescued. He did not think anything, left his mind blank. There was nothing to think. Just the storm outside and the girl-woman who had almost died but who had come back.

He was extremely tired and as soon as the shelter—drummed into noise by the wind and blown snow—had warmed and the meat had reached his stomach he couldn't hold his eyes open.

He slept sitting up—or didn't sleep so much as close his eyes—and ceased to be in the tent.

His mind slid sideways into the dream.

13

The Dream

THE STORM had cleared but it had taken days, many days. Too many days.

The man got the dogs up, up out of stiffness and the frozen positions they had taken in ice. One got up and fell over, too far gone to live. The man used his spear and the quick thrust to the back of the head to kill the dog. Its feet were frozen and it would have been in agony if he had tried to keep it alive. When it was dead he threw the carcass on the sled to feed the other dogs later.

Then he made them go. They did not want to leave, they were stiff with cold, but he whipped them and made them go.

Across the strange dreamgrass and dreamsnow they moved, the bone and ivory sled starting slow and pulling hard. He stopped and urinated on the runners, using a piece of hide with hair on it to smooth the new ice, and the sled pulled much easier.

And now, where the land had been open and barren, there was much game for the man. He passed herds of caribou, once another mammoth which had died and was frozen, with giant wolves tearing at it.

The wolves watched him pass. Two of them made a small sweep toward the sled and the man— there were times when they would have killed and eaten both the man and the dogs—but there was much easy meat on the mammoth. They turned away without making an open threat but it wouldn't have mattered.

The man almost did not see them. He had one purpose now, driving the lined-out team in front of him. Down to four stiff dogs, but loosening by the mile, he ran them out. The whip cracked and cracked again, reaching out to flick meat from their backs, meat and tufts of hair that flew into the cold, and they ran for him.

They ran for home.

Across the white land they ran, across the whiteness that was so bright in the dream it turned at last into light. Whitelight with the dogs churning through the brightness, legs slamming forward and down, feet kicking up snow, day into night into day into night into day . . .

The dreamdogs ran in the dreamworld across the whitelight until finally in the great distance they disappeared and out in front of what they were, what they had become, Russel could see the space where the tent was in the dream.

But it was the tent space only.

Torn leather, ripped skins that flew and flapped, tattered banners in the never-ending arctic dream-wind.

Where there had been a place of life, a place of laughter and round fat faces, where there had been a place of things that meant home and living, there was only the bleak shreds of flapping leather and the signs of death.

An end to things.

No, Russel thought—out of the dream but still in it in some way he did not understand. No, that cannot be.

But it was. In the dream it was. There was an

end that came in the north, an end that came to all things, the same end that came to Oogruk. The wolves had come, and when they were done, the small white foxes had come, and where there had been a woman and two children, where they had ended their lives, there was nothing.

Two bones.

Neither of them was identifiable except as bones, but they were human because they had not been cracked for the marrow and if they had been left from meat the woman would have cracked them to eat of the marrow—one small and the other large and long.

Two bones.

They were in the space that used to be tent but they were all. Everything else, every little thing that would have meant life and home was gone.

Even the lamp.

But only a small distance to the north, under an overhanging ledge, the lamp lay. Russel saw it. A fox had taken it there; drawn by the smell of fat that for years had soaked into the stone, it had taken the lamp under the ledge to get away from the other foxes and had licked the fat-smell until even that smell was gone.

Then it had left the lamp and trotted away.

It was a shallow stone lamp, with a flat bottom

and a groove in the edge where the moss wick would lie.

The dreamlamp lay where the fox had dropped it, lay until the blowing wind would cover it with snow and the snow would make grass and the grass would cover it still more, and then the snow and grass would, each after the other, time after time, mat the lamp down where it would lie forever. Or until somebody came to move it.

The lamp, Russel dreamthought. Not all that was left . . .

Another shift came; the dream moved sideways once more and he saw the man. Into the night and back to day the man had driven the sled until the dogs were staggering, falling. They were run down so far they would die surely. There would not be a team when the man was done—there would be only dead dogs.

Nothing but the man would be left.

They had run through the light, through the dreamlight the dreamdogs had run until they were no more.

Until there was only the man and the sled and where the tent had been flapping in the wind, only tattered pieces of tent.

And the man was Russel and Russel was the man. He knew that the woman and two children were no more and that the dogs would be no more and that's when Russel awakened in his own tent and saw the lamp.

Saw the flickering lamp and felt himself bathed in the stink-sweat of fear and knew, knew in his center, that it was the same lamp and that it was all there was left of what had been.

That's when Russel awakened in his own tent and knew that there was not a line any longer between the dream and the run.

That's when Russel awakened in his own tent stinking of fear and sweat, knowing that the dream had become his life and his life and the run had become the dream and the woman was looking at him.

The woman-girl, girl-woman sat staring at him past the flickering yellow of the lamp.

And she was the same woman as the woman in the dream. The same round face of the girl-woman in the dream, the same hair, the same even mouth of the dreamwoman-girl, with the same wide nose and clear eyes staring at him through the flame-light.

The dreamflame.

From the dreamlamp.

14

The Dreamrun

At the other end of the dreamrun nothing was the same as when he started. At the other end, Russel was no longer young but he wasn't old, either. He wasn't afraid, but he wasn't brave. He wasn't smart, but he wasn't a fool. He wasn't as strong as he would be, but he wasn't ever going to be as weak as he was.

When he thought of what happened, later, when he wasn't what he would be but wasn't what he had been, he thought that in some mysterious way a great folding had happened.

The dream had folded into his life and his life had folded back into the dream so many times that it was not possible for him to find which was real and which was dream.

Nor did he feel that it was important to decide. In its way the dream was more real than the run, than his life.

These things happened. Either in the dream or the run, either in one fold or another fold, these things happened:

He came to know the woman-girl. She was named Nancy. She had become pregnant without meaning to, without being married, and because the missionaries had told her that it was a sin she had been driven by her mind, driven out into the tundra to die on the snowmachine.

But fear had taken her. She had been afraid to die and she had turned to go back—she did not know how far she had come—and she had run out of gas. She had started to walk, had gone down with the cold, was going to die and Russel saved her.

She had gone first out to sea and then turned inland so they would think she'd gone through the ice and would not look for her inland. She did not have parents to worry for her. Her baby was not due for four months but she had pain in the tent that first night and Russel worried, though there was nothing he could do for her.

They could not leave. The storm was too strong for them to leave. He fed her meat and fat from a caribou carcass, watching her eat and talk between mouthfuls, heating the pieces of meat and putting them in her mouth, holding back when she winced with pain as she came back from freezing, handing her the next piece when she was ready for it. He let her talk and talk, now that he was rested.

When at last she had settled and had stopped talking about herself she stared at him.

"What is the matter?" Russel asked. "Have you never seen people before?"

Nancy looked down, suddenly shy. "It isn't that. It just came to me that you were out here with a dog team. There is nothing out here. How did you come to be here?"

Russel thought of telling her of Oogruk, of the dream, of the run, but held back. That was part of his song and it wouldn't be good to talk about it before it was ready to sing.

Then he thought he might tell her of the lamp, but decided against that for the same reason. Finally he shrugged. "I am a person who is running north and came upon your machine. That is all." He did not tell her about following the tracks for so long.

"How far north?"

It was an impertinent question but he ignored the discourtesy. "Until I run to the end of where I am going."

And then she did a strange thing. She nodded, almost wisely. "I understand. But tell me, is it possible for a person to be with you when you run north to the end?"

It was a hard question to answer. In this run, Russel thought, in this run I thought I would be alone but it was perhaps not supposed to be so. It may be that is what the dream is telling me. That I am not supposed to be alone. If the dream is telling me anything.

Or another way of thinking: Is it possible to leave her out here? No. And still a third way: Would it be possible to take her home?

"There is nothing for me there," she said, shaking her head when he asked. "I have done wrong. There is not a way to live there. I will stay out here."

"And die," Russel finished for her.

"Yes."

"No." He shook his head. "You tried that and it didn't work. You became afraid and tried to get home."

"Not home," she corrected. "Back. I have no home."

"So."

"So."

"What am I to do?"

"Take me with you. I will earn my way. I can scrape the skins and sew them. I can make camp. I can feed dogs."

"Do you know dogs?"

"No. There were none left in my village. But I can learn."

And in that way she came to be with him when his life folded into the dream and the dream folded into his life.

In that way she came to be with him on the run.

Again during that long storm-night she slept and he dozed, but did not dream, and when he awakened this time there was light outside the tent and the wind had stopped. He reached outside and brought his parka in, scraped the ice off, slid it over his underparka and stood outside. He was stiff, worse than he'd ever been, so he stretched, felt his bones crack and creak.

The woman-girl put her anorak on and came out.

"It is cold," she said.

"Cold is our friend."

"I know. But I am not dressed as you. I feel it more."

"We will wrap you in skins in the sled. You will be all right."

She said nothing but nodded and began taking the tent down while he hacked meat off the carcass for the dogs. She put one skin on the bottom of the sled, curved up on the sides, with the hair in. The other three she put on top as a kind of blanket, with the fur inside. When it came time to go—after he had fed and brought the dogs up—she got in between the hides.

"There is comfort here."

He misunderstood. "I have never hauled anybody who is going to have a baby."

"I meant it is warm. There is nothing comfortable about having a baby."

"Ahh. I see."

The dogs were rested but stiff and it took them a mile or so to loosen up. But they settled into the routine of running; the leader knew that Russel wanted to cover distance and they ran.

The land was new. White-new with snow from

the storm and drifts from the wind and after a time the dogs were running up the sides of a white saucer into the light, running out and out until their legs vanished in light and the steam came back to Russel across their backs and turned them into part of the wind, turned them into ghost-dogs.

He stood the sled loosely, proud of the team, and he could tell that the woman-girl thought highly of them.

Out, he thought. Out before me they go. Out before me I go, they go . . .

They ran north, now two where there was one, ran north for the mother of wind and the father of ice.

And these things happened when Russel's life folded into the dream and the dream folded into his life:

It came that they ran past their food.

It was true that he perhaps fed the dogs a bit too much, but they were working hard and it took meat and fat to drive them. Three, four, seven more days of running north, stopping at night in the skins with the lamp and the chips of fat and the yellow glow while they ate much and talked little; sat in their own minds until they dozed and he came to know the woman-girl—eight, nine, ten days and nights they ran north toward the mother of wind, and they ran past their food.

The first and second day without food there was no trouble. The dogs grew weak, but when they didn't get fed they went back to work and began to use of the stored fat and meat of their bodies.

"They will run to death," Oogruk had said. "You must not let them."

At the end of the second day Russel's stomach demanded food and when he didn't feed it and ignored it his body finally quit asking for food and he went to work and began using the meat and fat of his body.

The woman-girl grew weak rapidly because her body fed the baby within. Russel saved the last of the food for her and when that was gone and it was obvious that the dogs could not go much further he stopped.

There had been no game. No sign. They had seen nothing and he was worried. No, more than worried—he had been worried when the first two days with no game sighted had come. Now he was afraid.

He had to make meat.

"I will leave you in the tent and take the team for meat. They will run lighter with only one person."

Nancy agreed, nodding. She got slowly out of the sled and pulled the skins out to make the shelter. They were near the side of a cut bank where a creek had long ago run. They used the dirt bank for one wall and made a lean-to.

There were some chips for the lamp, and a long strip of fat that he had been saving for fuel—pictures from the dream haunted him and he did not want to leave her without heat.

When the shelter was up he returned to the sled. "I'll be back."

It was as close as he would come to a goodbye and he made the dogs leave. They did not want to go. They thought they should sleep in camp and eat and saw no reason to go out again. But he forced them and when they were away from camp he made them run to the east, up the old creekbed. If there is game, he thought, it will be up the creek run.

But they went all of that day into the dark and he saw nothing. No hare, no ptarmigan, no tracks of anything.

With dark he stopped and lay on the sled in his parka. There was light wind, but not the vicious cold of the previous days of running. He tried to sleep but it did not come.

Instead he lay awake all night thinking of the woman-girl back in the tent. If he did not find game she would die.

She would die.

He would die.

The dogs would die.

Perhaps I ought to run back to her and kill and eat the dogs, he thought, over and over. If he kept running away from the shelter until the dogs went down he would not get back to her. If there was not game out ahead of him he would not get back to her. If he saw game but his mind was not true and the arrow flew wrong he would not get back. She would die.

She would die.

He would die.

The dogs would die.

But if he went back and they ate the dogs they would not be able to leave and they would die anyway.

And now when he thought, there was nothing from the ghost of Oogruk. No help. Nothing. Nothing from the trance or the time when they turned to yellow smoke.

Whatever decision he made, when the light came

back, it was *his* decision, just as going back to live the old way must have been *his* decision.

And when the light came across the snow he made the decision to go ahead to find game, knowing that if he was wrong they would all be wrong, the woman-girl, the dogs and all would be wrong and gone. Gone and gone.

In the second day he found nothing. Nor did he on the third day and now they had gone six days without eating and he felt weak. His eyes worked poorly and he ate snow so often that his lips were sore. Twice, then several more times, he thought he saw deer but when he got to where they had been there was nothing. Never had been anything. It was the hunger in his eyes, he found, that made him see things.

Finally the dogs stopped. They could pull no more, or so they thought. But now he remembered one more thing from Oogruk.

"The dogs run because they want to run," the old man had told him, "or because they *think* they want to run, or because you *make* them think they want to run. That is how to drive dogs."

And so now Russel drove them. He cut a whip from some willows in the old streambed and he laid it on their backs and they ran for him but it was wrong, wrong to drive them down that way and he knew that when he had whipped them and made them run and they went down there would be nothing left.

He would not get back to Nancy. His mind took that and made it part of him—he was failing. He would not get back. As in the dream, he would not get back and there would be only two bones left by the foxes.

Two bones.

And so he drove the dogs down, drove them the way the man in the dream had driven them and when his mind was gone, when there was nothing left of his thinking and nothing left of the dogs, he came around a bend in the old streambed and saw tracks.

At first he didn't believe them. They came off the left side of the bank and tore down into the snow at the bottom, breaking through the hard pack that had held the dogs and sled. He thought they were from the hunger in his eyes but when he got closer they did not go away.

They were huge.

And when he got still closer he saw that they were tracks of a great polar bear and that he did not believe, either, because the bear were hunted out for their white fur. Men used snowmachines and hunted them out and there were no bears.

But there were the tracks. And they were tracks of a great bear. And they had to be real because now the dogs caught the smell and took excitement. They increased speed but he knew that they could not last now.

And how to kill a bear?

Oogruk had said nothing.

The arrow would not be enough. He had the killing lance on the sled and he would have to use that somehow. He would have to catch the bear and use the lance to kill it.

A polar bear that was bigger than he, the team, the sled, the woman-girl and the tent combined—he had to take it with the small killing lance in the old way that nobody had used for so long that he didn't think there was a memory of it. Oogruk had never done it, or he would have told him.

The dogs went faster still and he was afraid that he would burn them out. He stopped them and let the right point dog loose—the one just in back of the leader on the right. He seemed to be the strongest dog and the most excited by the smell of the bear tracks. Perhaps he would catch the bear and keep it busy until Russel could get there and bring it down. Or try.

There was much doubt in him now about the bear, some fear, and more doubt. But the dog tore

away up the streambed and Russel took the killing
lance from the tie-down on the sled and loosened
the bow case and quiver.

Then he let the dogs take the sled after the loose
dog. They were clamoring to run—even though
weakened by hunger. They smelled it now, saw
him take up the weapons and knew that he would
try to kill soon and the sight made them crazy.

Up the old stream they wound, following the
tracks, faster and faster until at last they came
around a corner and there it was.

The bear had his rear back against the bank,
his head low and teeth bared. He was immense,
the largest bear Russel had ever seen, even in
pictures. The fur was dirty white, almost yellow.
It was an old male, with his teeth worn down,
but full of the winter death that makes a polar
bear so awesome. When he saw the sled coming
he raised on his hind legs and Russel's heart almost
stopped. The bear was a tower, a white-yellow
tower standing over the loose dog. The dog had
been dodging back and forth, trying to worry the
bear, but when the bear raised he went in to bite
at the white back leg. It was his last act.

The bear's head snaked down in a great curve
of power and his jaws closed on the back of the
dog and broke its back in a bite so savage that the

dog was dead before it could scream. Then the bear shook its head—a tearing shake—and the dead dog flew sideways in a spray of gore.

All in silence.

But now the bear rumbled in its throat and turned to Russel and the sled and the team. Here was an enemy, a thing to face, and it would face it and kill it.

But wait, Russel thought. But wait, bear. It is the same as the mammoth. There is sadness here for the same reason. A dog is dead. You will want the other dogs and you will turn your head sideways and the lance will enter you like light. But wait, bear. Wait for me. Wait for the sadness of your life that you must die to feed the man. Not all the time. But wait for the sadness this time, bear.

Russel took the lance and stood away from the sled and let the dogs go. They went for the bear in a pummeling scream, and with the same sharp movement the bear lowered on all fours and came for Russel.

The bear did not want the dogs. He wanted Russel. He wanted to kill the enemy standing with the little stick, kill the man. Kill the man-thing.

Russel felt a great calmness. He wasn't Russel. He was the man in the dream and the bear wasn't

a bear but the great stinking beast and Russel set
the shaft of the killing lance in the ground and
held the wide-ivory point at the right height to
take the bear at the base of his throat and now
the bear came and now the dogs swerved in to
take him and the bear's head went sideways for
the dogs and the bear, stinking with the same smell
as the beast in the dream, and now the bear had
his head sideways and now the lance entered.

Like light. It slid through the hair and the fat
and into the center of the bear, into the center of
the center of the bear and Russel screamed a savage roar of triumph and the bear was on him.

On him and over him, hitting him with a stun-
ning blow of his right paw even as the lance took
his life. Russel knew he had killed the bear, but
felt the pain and saw the flash as his own life
seemed to fly from him and he thought with a
violent clarity: but wait, bear.

But wait, bear.

And then he saw nothing.

And these things happened when Russel's life
folded into the dream and the dream folded into
his life:

When he came back into his life from where the

bear had knocked him away the bear was dead
and the dogs were chewing at his rear end and
Russel was underneath his left front shoulder, the
blood dripping down on him from where the lance
shaft had entered the bear.

He fought to get from under and crawl to the
side. When he could stand, his head aching and
dizzy, he looked down on the bear and felt his
heart go out of him and into the bear.

"Thank you. The meat will be welcome."

A sadness took him, because he had no food for
the bear. Such a bear it was, so big, but he had
nothing for him but the thought of food. It would
have to be enough.

The bear was a mountain of meat. It weighed
close to three quarters of a ton. More meat than
he could eat, than the dogs could eat in a month.
More even than the woman-girl . . .

He remembered her suddenly.

He would feed the dogs and take some meat
and go back for her. As fast as possible.

He used his knife to lift the back-end hide and
took a large chunk of meat from the rear leg. This
he fed to the dogs, who ate and puked and ate
again. Then he took another large chunk of fat
meat, which he put in the sled, and he turned
them and started back.

They didn't want to leave the bear. The meat had given them strength almost miraculously fast, but they didn't want to leave the kill. He finally had to get in front and drag the leader back down the streambed until they had gone around two bends and were well away from the dead bear. Even then they worked reluctantly for a time.

But he let them seek their own pace and kept them going and in two days—feeding them liberally from the meat as he drove them—they had come within sight of the tent.

It was day—clear and cold—and he saw the lean-to half a mile before they got to it. It was not tattered, but there was no steam coming from the opening at the top and he feared for her.

"Nancy!" He called her name when he came near the tent. "I am back . . ."

But there was no answer. He set the hook and grabbed the meat and ran for the tent. It took him just a second to lift a corner and get inside but he felt the cold immediately.

She was lying on her side, the end of a skin wrapped around her as a sleeping bag and she was either sleeping or dead or in a coma.

The lamp was out. The fat was gone. He took some from the bear, rich yellow fat, and cut pieces into the lamp. He found some moss and got the lamp going—as the first time, only with great difficulty.

The warmth came out from the flame at once and he opened the skin around the woman-girl to let the heat reach her.

When he moved her he saw her eye flicker and he thought: twice. Twice she has come back from death.

But this time she was not frozen, as she had been the first time, or not frozen to such depth. There was not that wrong with her. She smiled at him.

"I did not think you were coming back." She spoke in a whisper that was almost a hiss.

"I said I would be back."

She said nothing more. He cut meat in small pieces and heated them on the lamp and put them in her mouth and she chewed and swallowed and where there had been an end there was once more a beginning.

But worse was wrong. Worse than he thought could be.

Even with the meat she did not revive. She ate, but when he thought she should eat more she held back and she did not come up and because he had come to know the woman-girl he worried.

"You are sick," he said. Outside it was dark and

the wind was blowing again. Or still. "What makes you sick?"

She didn't answer at first. Then she grunted. "It is the baby. The baby is coming early. I cannot stop it."

"Ahh. That is not good, is it?"

"No." She turned away from him, face to the back of the tent. "Maybe you should leave me alone."

But he had run once, left her to go for meat and he would not leave her again. Leaving had torn him and he still thought of the dream and the tattered tent with the foxes. "I will stay."

She said nothing to this and he took that as acceptance—or perhaps she was too sick to argue.

"Is there a thing I can do?" he asked.

But again she did not answer. He put more fat in the lamp, pulled the wick up to make more heat, then went outside and fed the dogs. They would sleep for days now, he knew, and that was fine. He had enough meat to last a long time and by then they would be able to travel. If not, he could just go back to the carcass and get more. With a strong team it was only a day and a half away.

With food anything was possible.

When the dogs were fed and the meat pulled

back in the shelter, he felt the exhaustion come down on him and it was not possible for him to stay awake.

In the warmth of the lean-to he slept, the ringing, deep sleep of the utterly tired when it seems as if nothing can awaken the mind. His head lay back against her feet and he slept and thought he would not dream.

But a thing came. He could not say if it was a dream or if it was real. But a thing came to happen in that night that he knew—and if he knew it sleeping or knew it awake it did not matter.

Foldings:

The woman-girl became a woman in the night. She was quiet at first, but moving and throwing her body back and forth and then in the yellow of the lamp she gave short-sharp sounds, sounds from the center of her center.

And he saw-felt that.

She strained and heaved and pushed and in the folds of the skin and the agony of it was not something he understood but he knew the sadness because it was the same sadness somehow that killing the bear had been.

In his mind he tried to help her but he was not sure if he really did or only wished that he could.

And still she worked. The cries became closer

together, and shorter, and deeper, and then she screamed, and then a time, a lifetime of almost animal whimpers and another scream and the thing had happened and it was in his hands and there was not life in it.

"Take it away!" she screamed. "Take it away now. Before I see it. Put it away from me. Outside."

And either he did or dreamed he did or wished he did—he went from the tent with the baby and up on the hill in back of the tent and he walked in the cold and put it on the hill and he thought that he had never been so sad. A tearing sadness.

But there was not life in it. There was not life.

And when he got back to the lean-to or thought he did or wished he did she was either asleep or unconscious and he fell back on the skin and slept with her.

And he wished then that he had stayed in his village.

And these things happened when Russel's life folded into the dream and the dream folded into his life:

Nancy lay for five days in the lean-to while Russel fed her meat from the bear, warming small pieces on the end of a willow and handing them to her.

But there was some trouble he did not understand with the woman and soon she went back to being a girl-woman, looking small and pale, and when those five days had passed he knew they would have to go.

"You need help," he said. "From a doctor. We will have to go to a settlement."

She said nothing. Her face had taken on the yellow of the lamp but it was the wrong yellow, the kind of yellow that stayed even when he opened the tent flap and let the daylight in.

"Here is the way it is," he told her, though he was not sure she knew what he meant, or even that she listened. "I do not know for sure where we are or how far we've come. But I think it is closer to the north coast and a village there than it would be to try to get back to your village. We came a long way. My dogs are strong." Even now, he thought, even now it is hard to keep pride away. "So I think we will go to the carcass of the bear and get meat and fat and then run for the north. As before. It should not be far to the edge of the land and there will be a village as there are villages along the coast everywhere and there will be help for you." It was the longest talk he had made since finding her. "That is the way it is."

Still she said nothing. But she nodded so he knew that even weak she understood and had been listening and he felt better for that.

So began the race.

The dogs were strong almost past measuring. Though there were only four left they had been fed meat and run so their legs rippled and were hard to the touch. Their heads were also hard. They had seen and done much and now they knew the man on the sled, knew that he was part of them, knew that no matter what happened he would be there and that made them stronger still. The strength in them came back to Russel and he fed on it and returned it as more strength still.

We have fire, he thought as they left the camp and went for meat to begin the final leg of the run. We have fire between us that grows and grows. Fire that will take us north to safety, fire that will save Nancy.

So began the race.

They took meat from the bear, as much as Russel thought they could carry, but had to leave the hide, the beautiful hide, because it was too heavy. He took the skin from the front legs to make pants, but the rest had to stay.

She brightened when they reached the dead bear. "You did this," she whispered. "With a spear you did this?"

He looked away. "And with the dogs. A man does not kill a bear alone. The dogs helped."

"Still. It is a huge thing, is it not?"

And now he chose not to answer. The dead bear made him sad, doubly so because they had to leave so much behind. It seemed wrong to talk of it as being a big thing—killing the bear with the lance. He did not wish to speak cheaply of it, or brag of it.

So began the race.

They left the bear and headed north again, running in sun and light wind. In the dark and some gentle snow they ran; up the edge of the saucer of light they ran, day into day they ran for six days, stopping only to feed the dogs and rest them in three- and four-hour naps, sleeping on the sled— or Russel sleeping next to it and Nancy on the skins—then up and gone again.

I must win this race, Russel thought. I must win. The girl-woman named Nancy got worse, grew weaker, but his strength grew with her weakness, his strength grew and went into the dogs.

Now they had more light. Winter was still there,

but the sun was coming back and he ran through the sun, grateful for the warmth. Even the nights were not so cold.

The dogs did not go down now. They were everything he would have wanted them to be and he drove them with his mind, drove them to the edge of the land, drove them until he felt the land start to tip down and then he smelled it, finally saw the sea ice out ahead.

When he got them to the edge of the sea he stopped and leaned over.

"See? We are north. We have come to the edge of the land."

She was still, but the edges of her eyes were glowing with life, with happiness, with the pride in his voice at what his dogs had done. She was weak, weak and down, but there was still life, enough life, and the corners of her mouth turned up in a smile, a smile that went into Russel.

"See?" he said, raising the team. "We will be in a village soon."

And he brought them up and ran them with his thoughts and on the ice they cut a snowmachine trail and he followed it to the left because that is what his leader said to do and he was the leader and the leader was him.

They drove down the coast, drove on the edge

of the sea-ice and land-snow, drove into the soft light of the setting spring sun, drove for the coastal village that had to be soon; the man-boy and the woman-girl and the driving mind-dogs that came from Russel's thoughts and went out and out and came from the dreamfold back.

Back.

PART THREE

DOGSONG

Come, see my dogs.

Out before me
they go,
in the long line to the sea.
Out they go.

Come, see my dogs.

They carry me
into all things, all things I will be;
all things that will come to me
will come to my dogs.
I stand on the earth and I sing.

Come, see my dogs.

    See them, see them
    in the smoke of my life,
    in the eyes of my children,
    in the sound of my feet,
    in the dance of my words.
    I stand on the earth and I sing.

Come, see my dogs.

    My dogs are what lead me,
    they are what move me.
    See my dogs in the steam,
    in the steam of my life.
    They are me.

Come, see my dogs.

    I was nothing before them,
    no man
    and no wife.
    Without them, no life,
    no girl-woman breathing
    no song.

Come, see my dogs.

> *With them I ran,*
> *ran north to the sea.*
> *I stand by the sea and I sing.*
> *I sing of my hunts*
> *and of Oogruk.*

Come, see my dogs.

> *Out before me they go.*
> *Out before me they curve*
> *in the long line out*
> *before me*
> *they go, I go, we go. They are me.*